A Gaggle of Geese

A Joy Forest Cozy Mystery

Blythe Ayne

A Gaggle of Geese

A Joy Forest Cozy Mystery

Blythe Ayne

A Gaggle of Geese
Blythe Ayne

Emerson & Tilman, Publishers
129 Pendleton Way #55
Washougal, WA 98671

www.BlytheAyne.com
https://shop.BlytheAyne.com
Blythe@BlytheAyne.com

A Gaggle of Geese
ebook ISBN: 978-1-957272-20-7
Paperback ISBN: 978-1-957272-21-4
Large Print ISBN: 978-1-957272-22-1
Hardbound ISBN: 978-1-957272-23-8
Audio ISBN: 978-1-957272-24-5

[**FICTION** / Mystery & Detective / Cozy / General
FICTION / Mystery & Detective / Women Sleuths
FICTION / Mystery & Detective / Cozy / Animals]

BIC: FM

DEDICATION:

To All Who Believe in Miracles

Books & Audiobooks by Blythe Ayne

Fiction:

The Darling Undesirables Series:
The Heart of Leo - short story prequel
The Darling Undesirables
Moons Rising
The Inventor's Clone
Heart's Quest

Joy Forest Cozy Mystery Series
A Loveliness of Ladybugs
A Haras of Horses
A Clowder of Cats
A Gaggle of Geese

Novellas & Short Story Collections:

5 Minute Stories
13 Lovely Frights for Lonely Nights
When Fields Hum And Glow

Children's Illustrated Books:
The Rat Who Didn't Like Rats
The Rat Who Didn't Like Christmas

Nonfiction:

How to Save Your Life Series:
Save Your Life with the Dynamic Duo, Vitamins D3 and K2
Save Your Life with Awesome Apple Cider Vinegar
Save Your Life With The Power Of pH Balance
Save Your Life With The Phenomenal Lemon
Save Your Life with Stupendous Spices
Save Your Life with the Elixir of Water

Excellent Life Series:
Love is the Answer
45 Ways To Excellent Life
Life Flows on the River of Love
Horn of Plenty—The Cornucopia of Your Life
Finding Your Path, Engaging Your Purpose

Absolute Beginner Series:
Bed Yoga – Easy, Healing, Yoga Moves You Can Do in Bed
Bed Yoga for Couples—Easy, Healing, Yoga Moves You Can Do in Bed
Write Your Book! Publish Your Book! Market Your Book!

Poetry, Photography & Art:

Home & the Surrounding Territory

Audiobooks:

Save Your Life With The Phenomenal Lemon
Save Your Life with Stupendous Spices
The Darling Undesirables
The Heart of Leo

Blythe Ayne's paperback, large print, hardback books, ebooks & audiobooks
are found wherever books are sold.

www.BlytheAyne.com

Table of Contents:

Chapter 1
A Gaggle of Geese

M *adagascar!* Land of lemurs and baobab trees. I stood amid a virtual baobab forest, looking up at the towering trees, their bare trunks reaching up to their canopy far overhead ... when my computer had the temerity to interrupt.

"Incoming...."

I ignored it.

"Designated urgent," my computer dared to continue.

"*From who?*" It had better be pretty darn important.

"Sophia."

Sophia? What could she possibly have to say to me that was urgent? "Pause program. Connect with Sophia."

"Oh, Joy, I'm so sorry to bother you!" Sophia appeared in the holo among the exotic baobab trees. In her trademark flowing lavender clothing, she looked stunning, and the baobab trees appeared to approve of her presence. "I'm sure it's the middle of your workday."

Inwardly, I nodded. "You designated your call urgent?..."

"Very urgent, Joy, *yes!* You know the goose girl, and, well, the most terrible thing has happened—the most terrible thing! The statue has disappeared. Everybody is in a total state. I never saw such a frenzy at her place, as you can imagine...."

I. Had. No. Idea. What. She. Was. Talking. About.

"Dear Sophia, *what* are you talking about?"

There was a long pause. Then softly Sophia said in a voice laced with disbelief, "You … you … you don't know who the goose girl is?" Her bafflement knew no bounds.

"I haven't the foggiest notion, dear Sophia, who the goose girl is and, *what*," I paused. I restrained myself from adding an expletive in the pause, "s*tatue?* You've mentioned a statue I know nothing about and tell me it's missing. As you can see, I'm completely in the dark." I looked longingly at the faded baobab trees outlining Sophia, with the strongest feeling that yet another project would soon be seriously interrupted.

Sophia carried on in her vein of disbelief. "I cannot fathom how you can be a self-proclaimed researcher of the human family, and not even know about an important individual in your own, *practically literally*, backyard."

Duly reprimanded, I refused to feel guilty. "But Sophia, that very factor leads to my stunning ignorance. I don't *do* research in my own backyard." I waved to the baobab trees around her that she couldn't see. "I'm retained to do research on cultures in other parts of the world, you see."

"I don't see how that precludes you from being aware of what's in your immediate surroundings." Sophia frowned.

Hmmm... what I saw in my immediate surroundings were the baobab trees of Madagascar. But it would only add to the confusion to try to point that out. *Why* had Sophia called me, now hovering in my paused project? "I'm unclear, dear Sophia, as to why you've called."

"Goodness! It's so obvious. We need you to discover who stole the Goose Girl Statue."

Yet more confusion! "Is there a goose girl, or a Goose Girl Statue?"

"There's a goose girl, *and* there's a Goose Girl Statue. You're needed, Joy. You're very much needed *here*. Please come! People need their healing."

"Healing? I'm sorry, Sophia. I haven't been known for healing people."

"*Oh my goodness!*" Sophia sighed. "Of course, you don't heal, no one's asking you to heal! The Goose Girl Statue is what heals." Sophia talked slowly, like addressing a somewhat slow child. I wondered why she felt I was up to her assignment at all!

In any case, we'd gotten to the bottom of it, and I finally understood why she called. "Oh! I get it!

Sorry for being obtuse, I had my head in my work. I think I'm on the same page with you now. However, Sophia, I don't imagine I can be of much assistance."

But now, darn it, I was intrigued.

Who was this goose girl I'd never heard of that apparently everybody else knew?

And, *what* about this Goose Girl Statue, with the purported ability to heal?

Suddenly, the mystery became more intriguing than the beautiful baobab trees. "I'll come and check out the situation, but, as I say, I don't think I can be particularly helpful. I'm sure you've called the police."

"No, Joy. I called you first, of course! But if you insist, I'll call the constabulary."

"It's not for me to insist. Isn't that within the purview of the goose girl? The living goose girl. Not the statue goose girl. If that makes sense. Which I'm not sure it does. Anyway, where are you?"

"Ten-eighty-six, north two-hundred-and-second."

As she said it, the location came up on my holo, covering her face and my ever-receding baobab trees.

"That's a..." I started to say as Sophia clicked off. "*Church!*" I exclaimed.

Chapter 2
The Goose Girl Statue

Sighing in resignation, I got up and started to thrash about under the desk for my shoes.

"Are you looking for your shoes?" Robbie, my robot cat, asked. He'd been sitting by my chair curled up, almost like a bio cat, not only listening, but recording every word that had transpired.

"Yeah, I kicked them off, I think, here somewhere."

"No, Joy. They're at the back door."

"All righty then." I reached across the bed and petted my actual bio cat, Dickens. He opened a sleepy eye, almost purred, and went back to sleep. Robbie followed me into the kitchen, on my way to grab up my backpack and put on my shoes. "Car, come to the back door," I said into my wrist comp. I heard it pulling out of the garage.

"Okay, Robbie, I'll be back ... well, I don't know when. Pretty soon I imagine. I don't think this is anything that justifies my precious time, but it'll be nice to see Sophia."

"Can I come along?" Robbie begged. "Please let me come with you."

"No Robbie, I won't be gone long."

"I never get to go anywhere," he complained.

"That's because your job is to take care of the home. Anyway, it's not objectively true, is it?" I wasn't about to go into the various adventures we've been on outside of the home, when, in fact, I'd found it helpful to have him with me. He is, after all, my supplemental mind!

Backpack over my shoulder and shoes on my feet, I stepped out the door and into the car. "Ten-eighty-six, north two-hundred-and second," I told the car.

"Church?" Car queried. "On a Tuesday morning?"

"So it would seem. Sophia called and said I needed to come because some statue is missing. This is the address she gave me."

"Oh!" the car said, surprised. "The Goose Girl Statue!"

My car knew more than I. "You know about the Goose Girl Statue? How ... why... oh, I'm completely mystified."

"I'm surprised you don't know about the Goose Girl Statue. It's practically in our back...."

"Don't say it! So, Mr. Smarty Car, did you know the Goose Girl Statue is missing?"

"Oh no! That's bad for the local folks."

"How so?"

"Because the Goose Girl Statue is known to heal pretty much anything that ails a human. Really, how do you not know...."

"*Do not say it!* I heard it from the lovely Miss Sophia, and I sure as holy-hecky-doo-rue, do not need to hear it from my car."

"Yes, Dr. Forest. As you say. I hope you'll be able to discover the whereabouts of the Goose Girl Statue."

"*Hmmmm,* I doubt I'll become engaged in that activity. My deadline for the Madagascar project looms, and I mustn't be distracted. I'm going now out of a bit of curiosity, and I thought it'd be nice to see Sophia. In other words, I'm simply taking a short break."

"Oh. I see." The car had a tone of voice. He might as well have said, "I'll believe it when I see it."

"I'll not have that attitude from *you*, automobile. You're to drive, not to editorialize."

"Yes, Dr. Forest."

Did I hear a small chuckle, or was it just an engine noise?

No time to contemplate that as we approached a church nestled on the hillside with several hundred people milling about in the yard on the bright sunny day. It had the air of a country fair. Or a revival. Women in colorful, flowing garments stood in bevies like a flower garden gone wild. A few men dotted the landscape. Light sparkled off the church's stained glass windows. With hardly a place to park, my car pulled onto a bit of grass and stopped.

As I began to open the door, a gigantic gaggle of geese came flying and honking, their wings fully extended, directly toward me from across the yard. Was I about to be attacked? I closed the car door and watched the geese as they gathered around my car door, honking and flapping their gigantic, elegant wings.

Why their undivided attention to me, I could not comprehend. I heard my name being called. *"Joy! Joy! Come along!"*

I looked in the direction of the crowd, trying to see who had called to me, and then I saw Sophia.

I opened the door a crack. "The geese! They look like they're going to attack!"

She giggled melodically. "No, no, dear. They're a welcoming committee. They welcome everyone. They're happy to see you."

Cautiously, I opened the door and slipped out. The goose conversation augmented in volume. But they didn't attack. They gathered even closer around me, honking, and chatting, and wing-flapping. Indeed, they seemed as though they couldn't be happier to see me.

What amazing creatures! They flaunted their wings, extending them full length, their wingspans as much as eight feet across! I made my way among the massive bird bodies toward Sophia as she made her way to me, while the great goose gaggle welcoming committee continued their chorus at the tops of their voices.

So much commotion! Geese, and dozens of women in soft spring fabrics, with a few men looking on, self-satisfied, as if they'd invented the day.

As I tried to take it all in, a loud, reverberating sound overhead demanded everyone's attention.

Chapter 3
The Little Door

The Space XXX Roadster police vehicle hovered overhead, gently coming toward the ground with geese and people scattering. Yet there was not enough room for the vehicle to land safely, and it moved out to the road, then sighed to touch down.

Officer Jamison climbed out of the vehicle and walked up to me. "Hey, Joy, I got a missing persons report. Did you call it in? What's the situation?"

"Hi there, Officer Jamison," I nodded to her, wondering where Travis was, that he wasn't manning his precious vehicle. "No, I didn't call in the report. I believe my friend, Sophia here, called in the report," I gestured to Sophia and she nodded energetically. "But I don't think it's a missing persons report," I continued. "I believe it's a missing statute report."

"That's right!" Sophia confirmed. "I made the call about the missing Goose Girl Statue. Very serious matter!"

"Let me understand this properly," Officer Jamison said sternly. "There's not a person missing? There's a piece of statuary from a church missing?"

"Yes!" Sophia said. "An extremely important statue, which is why all these people are here. Because of the Goose Girl Statue. The healing, Goose Girl Statue."

Puzzlement embraced Officer Jamison's features. "A piece of missing statuary does not require the presence of an officer. This is an offense to be reported online, with an image of the missing statue attached, if available." Officer Jamison shook her head in ill-disguised irritation, even as a radio on her person demanded her attention. She was needed elsewhere. "Do you think, Joy, you can attend to this matter, and see to it the form is properly filled out?" she asked as she hurried back to the Space XXX Roadster.

"Sure Officer Jamison, I'll do that. Is Travis off duty?"

"Yeah, and I'm off duty after I answer this call that's coming in of an *actual* crime." She climbed into the Space XXX Roadster and took off in a flash.

For myself, the only thought I had was: *Ha, ha!* I was *not* the only person who had never heard of the Goose Girl Statue. *Neener, neener, all you know-it-alls, including my car!*

I turned to Sophia. "Dearest Sophia, it's so lovely to see you! But I must make the observation that you're lucky she didn't cite you for a frivolous police report."

"Well, I just..." Sophia exclaimed, unable to clarify what it was she "just" ... so offended that Officer Jamison didn't appreciate the importance of the missing statue. "The Goose Girl is not ordinary statuary!" She waved her hand, taking in the surrounding population. "These people are dependent on her!"

"So I see," I said. "But, like me, Officer Jamison was not familiar with the Goose Girl Statue. There are some of us who are in the dark."

Sophia linked her arm with mine and led me back toward the crowd. "Let me bring you into the light about the goose girl and the Goose Girl Statue."

We plunged into the midst of geese and colorfully dressed women with their few chaperone men. That's when I noticed that the women, in their various groupings and bunches, did not look happy. Consternation clouded their features, and I heard exclamations of disappointment raising up from them, criticizing Officer Jamison's brief appearance without taking action.

And then I saw the rest of the Ladybirds in their own little bunch. "*Oh! Joy! Here you are!*" they exclaimed as Sophia and I approached them. Statuesque Elvira, Elgin, Mary, and little Possum gathered around me. "*Joy!*" they exclaimed again, happiness and relief mingled in their musical voices.

"Joy! You'll discover who stole the precious Goose Girl Statue!" Possum declared, giving me a big hug.

I smiled down at her, returning her hug. "Let's not get ahead of ourselves. Do we even know for a fact the statue was stolen? Perhaps the owner has moved it, or maybe even sold it."

The chorus of gasps that arose from the musical Ladybirds let me know my suggestion was tantamount to hearsay.

"She would never do that! She would never sell the Goose Girl statue!" They muttered in agreement.

"We must find Star Moon," Sophia said. "I don't know where she got to in the midst of all this muddle."

"Yes, yes," the Ladybirds assented. "We must find Star Moon. Joy needs to talk with Star."

"Star Moon?" I asked, again thrown into the realm of the unknown. "Who or what is Star Moon?"

"You don't know who Star Moon is?" Elvira asked with incredulity.

Again with the disbelief of my stunning ignorance. "If Star Moon is a person, I do not, no, I don't know who she is."

"She *is*," Sophia affirmed, "the goose girl. That's to say, she's the owner of this animal sanctuary and the caretaker of the Goose Girl Statue."

"And," I asked just to be sure, "her name is Star Moon?"

"That's right!" Possum confirmed. "That's her actual birth name. Her last name is Moon, as well as her sister. The Moon sisters. Her sister is Goldie."

"Goldie Moon?"

"Umm-hum."

"All righty almighty," I noted, finally moving into the game plan. "Yes, it seems like chatting with Miss Moon would be a good idea." Again, I didn't feel the urge to become involved in this mystery as much as curious to meet the young woman with the celestial name.

"I saw Star a little while ago," Mary said. "She doesn't appear to be the least bit ruffled about the disappearance of the Goose Girl Statue. Calm as the proverbial cucumber, when everyone else is so upset."

"Yeah, I noticed that too," Possum affirmed. "I'd be so traumatized! I *am* traumatized, and it's not even my statue. Just thinking about all these people here who came for a healing, it's very sad and upsetting!"

"It would be, yes," I said. I realized now that I had to give some serious thought to what I was being told. There were a lot of people here who believed the Goose Girl Statue had healing properties, and this many people ... well ... perhaps there was something to it.

I reminded myself that this line of thinking—becoming personally involved in the situation—would mean my Madagascar project would be set aside. Bumped. Overlooked, disregarded, neglected, ignored, left in the dust, unnoticed.

Because that's what happened when I became involved in something in the "real world," instead of my wide world of literary production. I love my work. But ... I couldn't ignore the real world, with real people, and real creatures! The geese again gathered around me, honking and chattering and flapping their magnificent wings.

"*Oh! Oh! Joy!*" All the Ladybirds chimed together, "*The geese! The geese!* They adore you! They know you'll help find the Goose Girl Statue. Their beloved Goose Girl Statue."

"The Goose Girl Statue is beloved by the geese?" I asked in surprise. "How do you know that? I mean, how do they let you know that?"

"Because," Sophia said, "they gather in the sanctuary every night and sleep around her."

"Miss Star Moon allows that?"

"Of course!" Elgin answered. "The statue loves her geese around her."

"And," Elvira added, surprisingly answering my unspoken thought, "the amazing thing, I add delicately, is that they remove themselves to the outdoors to attend to their bodily functions, and never soil the floor in the sanctuary."

"Amazing!" I declared. "All right then, let us discover the whereabouts of Miss Star Moon."

"I think she must be in the sanctuary," Sophia said.

I headed for the main double doors of the church.

"Wait, Joy." Sophia gestured to a small, unassuming door on the side of the church. "We generally use this door."

I nodded and followed her, not wanting or needing to go against convention. I came up to Sophia, and we stepped through the little door into a darkened space where I could see nothing other than Sophia's bright lavender, flowing clothing. I followed her as we came to a small group of people, whose outlines I could barely make out.

Someone spoke too softly, and I strained to make out the words, when suddenly a flash of light such as I had never seen in my life, rendered me blind.

"*Aughh!*" I cried, clapping my hand over my eyes.

Chapter 4
A Blinding Flash of Light

"**W**hat's wrong?" Sophia asked in a whisper. *"The light!"* I whispered back. *"The blinding light."*

The soft whispering I had been straining to hear became silent. Still holding my hand over my eyes, I peeked down at the floor, then removed my hand slowly. Darkness surrounded me as I was still somewhat blinded by the flash of light. I heard the soft whispering voice say, "Dear friends, I'm going to ask you to step outside for a few moments while I chat with my new friend."

I felt a hand on my elbow, and realized the voice referred to me as the "new friend." Sophia, and the several other people present, silently shuffled to the little door and went outside.

I didn't want Sophia to leave me, and I was surprised she did so without even a comment.

As my eyes adjusted, I became aware of a gentle, glowing golden light radiating around me, and a small, plain-as-a-pike-stick, woman in a flower sack dress that barely came to her knees, in bare feet, with a mass of dishwater blonde hair, looking as if it had never been brushed in this particular lifetime, stood before me beside an empty stand. Light flowed in pastel hues about the stand.

"Did you see the light?" she asked softly. "Did you see the flash of light?"

"Yes," I answered simply. "A blinding light."

"Then you've come!"

"I don't know what you're talking about. You must have me confused with someone else." Right, I thought, someone *else* who saw a blinding light, that, I guess, no one else who was here, saw. *Hmmm.*

The woman laughed a lovely, bell-sounding, charismatic laugh. "I don't think so. I don't believe I have you confused with anyone else. Do you see this light now, the one that comes from the statue's stand?"

"I do. I see a light in pastel hues flowing around this empty stand. Don't you?"

"Yes. Of course, *I* see it, but it's not usual for people to see the pastel hues." She gestured to the sanctuary behind me. "People see the lights from the beautiful stained glass windows, and that light is adequate for them to make their way around in the sanctuary, to the extent that they need to."

I turned around, surprised to see the entire sanctuary, and all the tidy wooden pews, in dazzling and brilliant shades of streaming colored light from the stained glass windows.

"Oh, my! I didn't even see this light when I came through the little door. I only saw that blinding flash of light."

"I know." She sat down on the floor. "Join me, will you?"

When in Rome, I thought, lowering myself to the floor in front of her, where I sat in the glowing light. That's when I saw the light also emanating from the tiny woman, herself. "Are you Star Moon?" I asked. Knowing, of course, she had to be. Even though unassuming, she had a powerful presence.

"I am."

"I'm Joy Forest. My friend, Sophia of the Ladybirds, perhaps you know her, insisted I come...."

"I know her very well and the beautiful, musical, Ladybirds," Star acknowledged. "It was thoughtful of her to bring you in here."

"She did more than that. She called me and told me the Goose Girl Statue was missing, and apparently, this is a rather big deal."

"Not as big a deal as most people are making it out to be."

"Let me say plainly," I noted, "that I'm completely in the dark. I can't say that I understand anything that's going on. But my friends insist that the Goose Girl Statue has been stolen. They also insist that this piece of statuary has the ability to heal."

"Your friends are mostly correct. The Goose Girl Statue does indeed have the ability to heal. However," Star gestured at the empty stand. "The statuary has left a residual light that is as healing as the statue itself."

"Oh, I see, and that's why you don't seem to be too upset."

"That's right. I'm not upset, because the sanctuary still provides healing for those in need."

"But, Star, where is the Goose Girl Statue? That's still the question. If she's missing, and you didn't move it, then someone took it."

"That's not how I see it." She reached out and stroked the statuary's stand.

"How do you see it? I'm confused."

"How I see it is the Goose Girl Statue apported."

"You mean, the statue moved from here on its own accord, somehow. It disappeared from this spot, and has appeared somewhere else?"

Star nodded. "That's right."

"Well then, if the statue has moved from here, where did it move to? Wouldn't it be important to find that out, in order to ally all the suspicions arising around it being stolen?"

Star shook her head, a small frown crossed her features. "Unfortunately, so far, the Goose Girl Statue has not let me see where she is. I don't know if she will. I believe there's a good possibility she returned to where she came from, which is India. And, as you know, India is a very big country. If she doesn't mean to be found by me, she will not be found.

"Anyway, I have faith that she has taken herself to where she's needed more than here. And again, although I miss her physical presence, she left powerful healing energy in this light." Star waved her hand through the beautiful, flowing, pastel light.

As much as I wanted to honor her beliefs, and as much as I felt I couldn't *argue* with what she believed, and as much as I'm probably more willing to accept events considered paranormal than the average bear ... I still had a niggling feeling that the statuary had been taken by human hands.

Did I dare say this to the mystical little Star before me? I did. "I appreciate your belief system, and, I'm not going to say I don't believe you. Perhaps you're right. But ... I have this feeling, my own sixth sense, that someone took it. Do you not perhaps share that feeling, at least a little bit?"

Star shifted about. "I am neither going to say I strongly disagree with you, nor that I feel you're correct. What I *do* believe, is that whatever the truth is, at *this* moment, it's serving to let everyone experience the lesson they are meant to experience." Star stood up. "This includes you, dear Joy. You, who I saw in a vision coming through that very door." She gestured to the little door through which I'd come. "In a bright light, just as you described.

"Whatever lessons there may be to learn, also include me." Star leaned forward and gave me a big hug, which took me a bit by surprise, but it felt so amazingly warm and with a healing energy of its own, that I received it wholeheartedly.

"What a great hug!" I exclaimed.

Star giggled the cutest little fairy-like giggle, then took my hand. "Let me show you something you may find curious and interesting."

"Oh! I'm always up for curious and interesting!"

I followed Star out of the main sanctuary and through a labyrinthine and dark path into the bowels of the church. We came to another little door—the church seemed to like little doors. Star opened the door to a room slam-jam packed with statues and religious artifacts. The energy from the room poured through the open door as if it had been waiting and waiting for someone to come along and release some of the energy.

"Is this not amazing?" Star asked simply. "Do you feel anything?"

I sighed, "Oh, my!" I moved into a small space inside the doorway. "Yes. I feel quite a lot. *Holy guacamole!* Do churches generally have a storeroom full of a variety of artifacts from different religions? Did you collect all of these?"

"Oh goodness no. I have neither time, nor money, nor inclination to collect, well, anything, actually. I have creatures and gardens and people to take care of. No, these artifacts were here, collected by the pastor, the previous owner of the church. He sold the church to me when his congregation either transitioned or moved away.

"He'd hoped to sell the church to another congregation, but no one showed interest. I was interested the first time I saw the 'For Sale' sign. It's a big piece of property and I knew it would be perfect for an animal sanctuary. At first, he didn't care for my idea, but eventually, I won him over and he sold me the church, the church property, and everything on it, as it stood, with the exception of these religious statues. They remain here, but they belong to him.

"He traveled all over the world and gathered these powerful artifacts. My agreement with him is that he can come here anytime he desires, because, although he really cares about this collection, he has no place to keep it in his current living situation. Every now and then I'll see him quietly leaving by the other little side door.

"The property is three-and-a-half acres and has been perfect for my animal sanctuary. Out back there lives quite a variety of rescued creatures. Several volunteers come early every other morning to help me take care of them."

"My goodness," I said, "you need to meet Evanora Montana."

"Oh," Star smiled and nodded, "I know Evanora very well! But this whole healing the human family concept is a new commitment in my life, which I've come to embrace. Though my natural energies are more aligned with animals, I've become more comfortable around people, in the process of seeing them become healed.

"It has been a main feature of my journey, to not have a prejudice against people. Creatures and humans, we are all much the same. Pain hurts a tiny duckling the same as it hurts a big, hulking, strong, man." She stepped out of the little room. "You're welcome to stay here if you'd like."

"No, not just now. But," I looked over my shoulder as I stepped out of the room, taking in a poised, mysterious energy that seemed to want to follow us out into the world, the sunny day, the spring flowers. "But, I would probably like to come here again sometime and sit quietly with all this energy."

"Any time, Joy, any time. You need not even tell me you're coming. I suspect I'll know it, anyway." She closed the door with a click. "Zev says I should sell these artifacts. He doesn't understand their significance."

"Who's Zev?"

"Ahm, he's sort of, I guess, one might say, my boyfriend." Star seemed uncomfortable with the notion, which she immediately confirmed. "I've never had a relationship quite ... this ... meaningful to me. I've been perfectly happy, taking care of creatures, which I've done ever since I first found a wounded baby rabbit at the age of three. It has kept me occupied.

"Anyway, Zev heard about the healing in my sanctuary and he came with a malady he had. As improbable as it seems, we struck up a conversation, and things evolved." Star paused. "My sister doesn't approve of him. But that's to be expected. I'm her little sister, and she's protective."

"Why is it improbable that you and he would strike up a conversation that grew into something else?" I wondered aloud. "You're extremely engaging and charming."

"You're very kind. But two more unlikely people finding one another you've probably never seen," Star replied. "Zev is very... very... well he's beautiful, he's a male model, and all very ..." she waved her hands around her body, "very fussy about every single tiny nuance of his appearance." She giggled her little fairy giggle. "It does make me laugh when he has to look in a mirror and see his hair one more time. Goodness! Beautiful boy, your hair is perfect, relax! I'll be thinking. I'm sure the fact that I haven't paid the least attention to my hair ever in my life is a big irritation to him. But, spirit will have its way! It has to do with more than hair, does it not?"

I laughed. "One hopes it does!"

I couldn't deny that Star possessed a compelling, charismatic quality, despite her scruffiness, her understated presence, her quiet nature. Beyond what she presented on the surface, there resided an ancient soul. Perhaps a bodhisattva.

I followed Star as she wended her way back through the church. "But, why such a big crowd on a Tuesday?" I asked.

"Tuesday just happens to have become the 'healing day.' I don't quite know how it came about, but it has grown of its own accord. Despite people's despair over the disappearance of the Goose Girl Statue, today has been a good day. Many people experienced miracles, right there where we sat."

I wanted this to be true. And why would it not be true? Miracles were simply events that had not yet been explained by science. I keep the attitude that anything is possible.

But I persevered. "The Ladybirds feel the statue has been stolen. They want me to look into it. How do you feel about that? I mean, you are the keeper of the statue, and you have a belief about it. But what if, in fact, it *has* been taken by someone? Wouldn't it be wrong for them to have it, when it belongs in this church?"

Star shrugged. "I don't mind if you're inclined to look into the possibility that the Goose Girl Statue was taken. But, I have no inclination to engage in that activity myself. She is where she means to be."

We now stood in the heart of the sanctuary, with the translucent colors of light from the stained glass windows pouring in, co-mingling and dancing all about, when a huge, throaty vibration shook the entire building.

Chapter 5
Rose Petal Tea

W e scurried out through the little door, just in time to see Travis in the Space XXX Road-ster settle on the ground. The crowds had dispersed enough for it to safely land, while the few people and geese nearby scattered in a dozen directions.

"Hey, Joy," he said, as he got out of the roadster and came over to me.

Heavenly Tuesday morning! I couldn't help it, the sight of him stirred my little pitter-pattery heart.

"Hey, Travis, I didn't expect to see you here."

"When I saw Officer Jamison's report, I thought I'd better come and check it out because, you know, where Joy is, there's usually something more to it than what appears on the surface."

I glanced over at Star. "I don't think there's much more than what you saw in Officer Jamison's report. There's a religious statue missing that belongs to this lovely woman by the name of Star Moon."

Travis nodded at Star. "Miss Star Moon, I have heard of you, and your supposedly healing statuary."

"*You have!?*" I asked, stunned.

"Right. A member of the office staff was proclaiming a miracle a while back after he had broken a bone in his foot. He'd been hobbling around on crutches for a week, and then suddenly no crutches, no hobbling. I asked him what happened, and he told me about his Goose Girl Statue miracle."

"So you believe in it?" I asked, a little bit in shock. He and I were always going around on things that had their underpinnings and dimensions in other than the three that are taken for granted. Travis was inflexibly grounded in the "real world."

"Anyone who knows you, Joy, has to be open to unexplained possibilities."

"*Woo hoo!*" I exclaimed. "A win for the paranormal!" I grinned, feeling pretty self-satisfied. Out of the corner of my eye, I saw a veritable cloud of pastels and wings coming toward us.

The Ladybirds and the gaggle of geese were converging upon Travis.

He followed my gaze. "*Whoa!*" He muttered at the sight.

"Whoa, indeed," I agreed. Quite the sight! The tremendous wingspan of the birds, embellished with pretty women in billowing clouds of pale green, pink, blue, yellow, and lavender, was breathtaking.

"*Huh-huh-huh-huh-huh,*" the geese chattered, as they scurried up to us. Star reached out and petted each in turn on their lovely heads.

At the same time, the Ladybirds all gushed over Travis. "Oh! Officer Rusch! It's delightful to see you! We're glad you're here!"

One would have thought he'd come to the party event of the season, instead of simply doing his job.

I looked at Travis, who manifested his crooked and irritatingly endearing smile. "Ladies, lovely to see you as well, even though this is not a social visit. I'm following up on the report regarding the missing statuary. Do any of you have an insight as to the disappearance of the so-called Goose Girl Statue?"

The five Ladybirds exchanged looks—meaningful, fraught with unspoken conversation, looks. Then they each looked at Star, and I understood that they did indeed have strong suspicions, but didn't want to voice them in front of her.

I saw that Star understood it as well as I did. "Say what you have to say," she said, the slightest edge of testiness in her voice. "We might as well clear the air here and now."

A pregnant pause ensued, but finally, Sophia spoke up. "Dear Star, we may be wrong. It might be better if we keep our mouths shut." She looked at her peers, who all looked down at the earth. Possum shrugged.

Then Sophia continued. "I guess the important question right now is, what do *you* think happened to the Goose Girl Statue, Star?"

Would she say what she believed, right now in front of the Ladybirds and Travis, I mean, *the law*?

Yes, she was.

"I think I know the energy of the Goose Girl Statue better than anyone here, and I'm pretty sure that with her power, she apported herself somewhere where she is more urgently needed."

"Apported!" Travis and the Ladybirds chorused together.

"Yes, apported," I said, feeling, perhaps unwisely, defensive of Star's belief.

Travis gathered himself from his exclamation of surprise and became coldly professional. "If I understand correctly, it's your belief, Miss Moon, that the statuary has some kind of paranormal ability to move itself."

"Yes."

"And why, Miss Moon, do you more believe the statue moved itself, than that someone took it?"

"Because there remains a healing light on her stand. It seems to me, if someone stole her, she would not have left a light. But she knows there's so much healing here, and she left her healing light to continue her work, even though she needs to be somewhere else."

"Interesting logic," Travis said, in the most un-readable tone of voice I've ever heard from him. He wasn't wrong, it *was* interesting logic. "But let me ask you this, Miss Moon, can you imagine even a remote possibility that someone took the statue?"

"Of course, there's a remote possibility. I am neither a dummy nor delusional, even though you may think I'm both. It's possible someone took the statue."

"So," Travis continued, "in that vein of logic, would you mind terribly if I listen to the suspicions of your friends? It's obvious that they care deeply about you, and only have your best interests at heart. Am I right?" He looked at each of the Ladybirds in turn. I watched as each of them melted just a little in his direct glance. *Ah!* I was not the only one he had this effect upon.

The Ladybirds all nodded and exclaimed with enthusiasm in the affirmative. "We only want what's right for Star! We only want the Goose Girl Statue back in her place! You're absolutely right, Officer Rusch, we care about Star, and we care about the goose girl healing people."

"All right then, let's hear your thoughts."

Once again, they fell silent. Finally, little Possum spoke up quietly. "I think we believe, *ahm,* that's not right, *ahm*, we think, or, we *wonder* if Zev doesn't have something to do with it."

"That's what I thought you thought!" Star said. She kept her cool, but anyone could tell this did not make her happy.

"Who is Zev?" Travis asked.

"He's my friend," Star answered. "And, just because we seem like a profoundly improbable couple—and nobody knows that better than me, because he's gorgeous, and ... I'm not...."

Protests arose from the Ladybirds. "No, no, no, Star. That's not true!"

"It's just," Elvira began, "he's not spiritual, he's worldly and self-involved, and, you know ... nothing like you. You're so amazing! So centered, so calm, so caring about the earth, and creatures and plants, and everything. We just ... we don't think Zev is good enough for you. We can't help observing that he appeared on the scene, and not long afterward, the Goose Girl Statue disappeared."

"A statue," Sofia continued, "that's worth a lot of money."

"*Hmmm,*" Travis mused. "When you say a lot of money, what do you mean?"

"Given that the statue is around fifteen hundred years old, a rare artifact, amazingly beautiful, and also, incidentally, has the ability to heal, its worth is virtually limitless."

"Oh! That does put a spin on the situation," Travis observed. "On what authority do you say this, Sophia?"

"I'm a volunteer curator for the National Art Conservancy. I ascertain the value of rare art and cultural artifacts on a regular basis."

"*Really?!*" Travis and I burst out. We exchanged a look.

"That's significant," I observed.

"Did you know the Goose Girl Statue was, essentially, invaluable?" I asked Star.

"Not to this extent, but it doesn't surprise me. The value people put on things is confoundingly mysterious to me. But in this instance, it would simply be intelligent to understand that the Goose Girl Statue is beyond value."

"Zev. Zev," Travis said reflectively. "That wouldn't be Zev Zarhan, would it?" Travis asked, frowning slightly.

I knew this expression on his face. It could not be good news.

"Yes," Star affirmed. "It is." She shook her head ever so slightly. "And, yes, I know he has a criminal record. He told me himself. Which wasn't necessary, because I intuited it anyway."

"And still, you do not suspect him?" Travis asked.

"No. I don't. In the same way, I intuited he has a criminal record, I also intuit he has not taken the statue."

"Who else do you suspect?" I asked the Ladybirds. There was something further they were not saying.

"We hate to say this even more than pointing a finger at Zev," Mary said. "But it has to come out. We sort of suspect your sister."

"*Goldie?*" Star said, truly surprised. "Why would you suspect Goldie? Honestly, that's a reach. She wouldn't do *anything* to hurt me."

Mary nodded. "That's absolutely true. She wouldn't do anything to hurt you. She'd do anything to take care of you. If she had even a clue of the tremendous value of the Goose Girl Statue, she might sell it to use the funds to take care of you."

"My goodness, that's a new one," Star muttered, probably as close to disgust as she'd ever been.

Oddly, I could see this struck a chord with her. Was it possible her sister *had* fenced the Goose Girl Statue to be sure her sister had enough to live on? I thought about the room *full* of religious artifacts in the dark recesses of the church. It probably contained enough value to support anyone comfortably for a couple of lifetimes.

But I felt it a pity to fence the Goose Girl Statue for that purpose, if that's what had been done.

Star shook her head. "I appreciate your concern, and I'm listening to your thoughts. But, if the statue has been stolen, why does it have to be by someone I care about? Why couldn't it just as well be some complete and total stranger?"

She had us there. She probably left the church open twenty-four-seven, so that anyone who needed a healing could visit the Goose Girl Statue. Or open for anyone inclined to thievery.

"That *is* possible, of course," Travis said. "It's entirely possible."

"And with that," Star said, "let us leave off this dreary subject and share a pot of rose petal tea."

"Oh yes, let's!" The Ladybirds agreed. They all began to move toward the cluster of tables and chairs at the far end of the yard, with the geese excitedly chattering and fluttering along with the Ladybirds and Star.

"Coming?" I asked Travis, fully expecting him to jump back into the Space XXX Roadster and fly off. But he surprised me.

"For a few minutes, yes. There's something I'm still trying to get a bead on."

"Oh? What's that?"

"It's not shaped in my mind enough just yet to discuss. I want to continue to observe a bit more."

"*Aaaand*," I added, "bonus! Rose petal tea!"

"Yes," he replied in a dubious tone. "Rose petal tea. *Hmmm*, it sounds a bit iffy."

"You've never had rose petal tea?"

"Nope. I've never had rose petal tea."

"Well then, if you don't like it, I'll have your share."

"Agreed."

We came up to the group, and Possum said, "Sit here, Officer Rusch." She patted the chair beside her. And then she patted the chair on the other side of her. "And, Joy, you sit here, on the other side of me."

Although there wasn't any reason to not sit there, I'd hoped to sit by Travis in case we needed to have a bit of a slightly private conversation.

A bit of private conversation? Who was I kidding?

Everyone rallied around, pulling up another little table and several chairs close to us.

I looked over my shoulder and watched Star enter the back of the church. *That's* when I realized—recalling following her through the church and having noted the large kitchen we passed—that Star *lived in the church.*

And why not? A huge kitchen, several bathrooms, and lots of Sunday school rooms for various interests or for little rescued creatures to recover in. It made a perfect home for Star and her creatures.

And then I had another *aha!* Something she'd said suddenly clicked. I jumped up and turned to scurry into the church, when, at that precise moment, a Drago slid silently onto the grass, and sighed to the ground.

Chapter 6
The Wonders of Love

I'd never seen a real Drago. Of course, "real" Dragos had only been in existence for about six months. Low, and sleek, and black—all Drago's were black, and black only. What an impressive vehicle to behold! As everyone was seated, and energetically engaged in conversation, no one but me saw the Drago silently arrive.

Dying of curiosity to see who would emerge from the velvety vehicle, I had a strong suspicion. The door slid up and out stepped a man a bit too gorgeous for plain reality. This had to be Zev. At the distance, even though I could tell he was movie star beautiful, he seemed a bit too small. I chalked it up to the distance.

I watched him size up our group and then make eye contact with me. He looked around, as if confused, and even as though he might turn around and leave.

"She's in the church, making rose petal tea for us," I called to him.

"Do you mean Star?" he called back.

The chatter fell silent as everyone turned to see who I was talking to.

"Yes, I mean Star, of course. We're having a little chat while waiting for her. Won't you join us?"

He hesitated. He even half-turned toward his vehicle like he might get back in, and slide away. But then he paused. Star came out of the church carrying a large tray. He looked at her, but didn't move.

I went over to Star. "Can I be helpful?" I asked.

"Why, yes, Joy. Thank you so much. I have another tray to bring out. If you take this one to the table, I'd appreciate it." She handed me the tray, while looking at Zev without uttering a word.

It was kinda weird.

"I'm assuming this is Zev," I said.

She nodded, continuing to stand where she was. "Hey, Zev."

"Hey, Star," he replied, also continuing to stand where he was.

"I invited him to join us, but he seems undecided."

"I came to see *you*, Star."

"I'm glad," Star said.

"Well ... I'll just ... leave you two ... to your scintillating conversation, and take this tray to the table," I said, moving off.

They appeared to either not hear me, or to ignore me.

I took the tray to the table. It wasn't until I got there that I looked down to see what I'd brought. I saw a steaming pot of wonderfully aromatic rose petal tea, and several charming but mismatched cups and saucers, with an array of little demitasse spoons. I took on the role of hostess, pouring everyone a cup of tea.

Elgin, on Travis's other side, speaking sotto voce, was deep in conversation with him. I sure felt curious about what the subject was. He appeared entirely engaged, and I knew he wouldn't be unless it really *was* interesting. But I couldn't make out a word among the general chatter and thank yous to me for pouring the tea.

I saw movement out of the corner of my eye and watched as Star and Zev emerged from the little church door. Star carried another enormous tray, Zev shadowing her, without even offering to take it from her.

I don't care if he's beautiful, I thought, he's lost a bunch of points. I noticed he was only maybe an inch taller than Star, and she was barefoot, while he had shoes on. He was maybe five-foot-one.

When she came up to us, I saw on the tray beautiful little pink cakes, another charming array of mismatched plates, and a pile of napkins with little roses on them. She set the tray down next to the other tray.

"I made these little rose petal cakes to go along with the tea. I hope you like them." She set the plates out, then centered the tray on the table, while everyone grabbed a little cake.

"Goodness, Star," I said, "you're so talented!" I took my cup of tea, my demitasse spoon, my plate, and one of the few remaining cakes, then sat at the other table.

"Thank you, Joy," Star said, looking around for Zev. He stood off to the side, having the appearance of preferring to be anywhere but here. Gorgeous, but awkward. "Would you like some tea?" she asked him.

He shrugged. "I ... I... Guess so. Never had rose petal tea."

"Well, then," Elvira said, "now is the time. It's delightful."

Star gestured for Zev to take the empty seat by me, and somewhat reluctantly, he did so.

"I'm Joy," I said. "It's nice to meet you."

Continuing to look at the tabletop and not make eye contact, he said, "I'm Zev."

"So, Zev, how did you meet Star?"

"I ... I ... ahm ... was hurt, and I'd heard of the healing statue here. So ... I came. I didn't believe in it. I really didn't. But I had never been in such pain in my life, so I thought I had nothing to lose to check it out."

He became animated as he spoke and less self-conscious. Even though he didn't make eye contact, his charm began to shine through his shyness.

"And so it seems to you the Goose Girl Statue healed you?"

He finally looked at me. *OMG.* What amazing eyes! Huge, predominately brown, but with shards of intense green. I think I actually gasped a little. "It doesn't 'seem to me' that the Goose Girl Statue healed me. It's a fact. An unarguable fact."

I nodded, taken a bit aback by his sudden passion juxtaposed against his, moments previous, intense timidity.

"You must be so upset that the Goose Girl Statue is missing," I dared to suggest. Would he steal and fence the statue, when he believed it had cured him? Wouldn't a person want to keep such a precious item where it belongs, in case one needed it again?

"No. I'm not upset that the statue is missing. There's a light glowing where the statue had been. In that light, many people have said they've been healed. Star says the statue has gone where it's needed more than here. I can't say I understand this, but I don't understand how it healed me, in the first place.

"I'm not particularly complicated. I function very much in the three dimensions. And I only know to say *that*, because Star made the observation about me. Seems about right."

My wonderment grew regarding what attracted them to each other, given that the only thing they seemed to have in common was their height. "So, Zev, I see you have a Drago, it's gorgeous! What's it like to ride in?"

I won him over with that! His entire body language changed. He relaxed, sat back in his chair, pretended to sip his tea, and looked at me as if I'd become his pal. "It's a dream! It's not like riding in a car at all. It's like … it's like being in a spa whenever you go anywhere, there's this luxury around you. I love it!"

"I hope you don't mind my asking what you do for a living, to be able to afford a Drago?"

"No. I don't mind. I'm a model. Make tons of money. You may not have noticed I'm just a tad short, and I don't get every gig. But I get enough to live as I please. I got the face."

I nodded. "That's true." I grinned at his transparency. Facts is facts. "You definitely got the face. Does Star like riding in the Drago as much as you do?"

"So far, she's refused to get into it. She says it's an embarrassing waste of resources, and she doesn't think it's appropriate to own such a thing."

"Oh!" Given how much he adored the vehicle, it seemed like this conflict alone would be a deal-breaker. "So, how do you feel about that?"

He shrugged. "It's not the only territory where we have different opinions. But never mind that. There's something about her that resonates with me ... I've never encountered such a range of pleasant feelings with any other human being in my life." He ran his fingers through his incredible mane of gorgeous dark brown, golden highlighted, hair.

That's when I noticed all the women at the two tables were looking at him. And why not? He was a sight to behold. Every woman, that is, except Elgin, still engaged in a forehead-to-forehead conversation with Travis.

Holy hedgehogs! What had they gotten into? Trying to ignore the thought, I returned my attention to Zev. "Star *is* amazing. There's something about her that resonates with me, as well." I sipped my rose petal tea and nibbled at my little rose petal cake. *Whoa! Incredible!* I gestured at Zev's tea and cake. "You should avail yourself of these delights, Zev."

"Yeah, all right." Cautiously, he took a bite of the little cake and sipped the tea. A look of surprise crossed his features. "*Damn!* That's good!"

"You didn't expect it?"

"I did not. I've always thought tea had no flavor. But this blows me away." He wolfed down the rest of the cake and guzzled the tea in one fell swoop, as if the idea of parsing it out and having some two minutes from now was beyond comprehension.

Star still served everyone. She looked across at Zev's empty plate and handed him another little cake. He held out his teacup, which she filled with a secretive smile. They exchanged a couple of comments through eye language, as a sweet charge of energy passed between them.

Though my suspicions were stronger than ever, I found myself hoping and hoping *and hoping* Zev would not turn out to be the thief of the Goose Girl Statue. If he'd thefted other things in the past, so be it. But I'd match any bet that he was turning from who he'd been, to a man discovering in amazement the wonders of love.

As I mused on this thought, all the devices on Travis's person that could squawk, jangle, chirp, or talk went off, and he jumped up. "Gotta go! Great talk, Elgin, we'll have to return to the topic sometime." He glanced at me, "Talk to you later, Joy."

Off he strode, the Space XXX Roadster charging up.

Well, at least he acknowledged me, I thought, just a tad frustrated.

Or perhaps more than a tad.

Chapter 7
Mystery of the Missing Statue

Travis's departure pretty much broke up the party. All the little rose petal cakes were gone, and I felt certain the two teapots were empty as well. We got up and said our goodbyes, with hugs all around, and promises to *get together very soon*.

We always promised to get together very soon, but life being vicarious in the way that it is, that "very soon" often morphed into a situation like today when something beyond our expectation called us together.

I loved spending time with the Ladybirds, and I felt it a privilege to meet and get to know, at least a little bit, the wonderful person of Star Moon, and yes, it was intriguing to become acquainted with Zev.

But I could not deny that the most fascinating aspect of the day was to have learned about the Goose Girl Statue, to see and to sense her light and energy, even after she'd been stolen. I wished I had known about her before. I would have loved to see her, to feel her energy.

This thought alone, I knew, would compel me to try to find the statue. Did I believe it had apported? Did I believe it materialized somewhere in India, its original home? Did I believe the statue knew where it was needed, or had become homesick for its homeland?

No. Not really. Not that I couldn't have those beliefs, but, about the Goose Girl Statue, I still disagreed with Star. I had an unshakable intuitive feeling that the statue had been taken by human hands. I was going on my viscerals, like I usually did, because they were almost always right.

By the time I finally got home, shades of night were falling.

"Drop me off at the back door," I said to the car as we came into the driveway.

The car came to a stop and I climbed out. "Good night, Car," I said, heading for the back door.

"Have a good evening, Dr. Forest," the car said.

"Oh, thank you that's so sweet. How did you learn such good manners?" He made me chuckle.

"From you, where else?"

"I guess I didn't know I was so polite. You have a good evening too, Car. I won't be going anywhere else tonight. Have sweet car dreams." I stepped inside.

"Where have you been?" Robbie accosted me at the door. "I mean I know where you've been of course, I'm hooked up to your every move. But! You've been gone all day, and have had virtually nothing to eat, not to mention that you didn't bother to check in with me even once!"

"I'm sorry, Robbie, you're absolutely right. But let me tell you! I had the loveliest rose petal tea and rose petal cakes, made from real rose petals. That's what I had to eat. But not only that, I became acquainted with an intriguing mystery."

"As always! You can't seem to make a move without stirring up some mystery."

"I don't stir them up, dear Robbie. They already exist. I just become aware of them and try to solve them, which is what I want to be contemplating right now. I probably do need a bit of actual nutrition, though."

Robbie swished his tail, letting me know his displeasure with me. As if I hadn't already gotten that message. "I made a little lunch for you, which now is supper, as you're so late. The lentil soup is cold, and the sandwiches are a bit dried out, but there they are."

"Oh, Robbie, thank you!" I looked at the bowl of soup and plate of sandwiches on the counter.

"It's not so easy, you know," he went on, "without opposable thumbs. But the fact that I can command the kitchen to warm up a bowl of soup and open the refrigerator door for me is helpful. I washed my paws thoroughly beforehand, and with water, even!"

I stooped over and gave him a big hug. "What would I do without you?"

"A lot more work than you do now, with probably less nutrition."

I reheated the soup, then took my little meal to the table. Pulling out the chair beside me I patted it for Robbie to jump up and keep me company, then bit into my sandwich. "Oh wow, great sandwich! What is it?"

"It's the chickpea salad you got the last time you went shopping, that you haven't even opened."

"You're so clever. I completely forgot I bought it."

"I know. Never mind all that, tell me about the mystery around the Goose Girl Statue."

"I guess you figured out that much from my day's adventure. The Goose Girl Statue apparently has miraculous healing abilities. Dozens of people were there when I arrived, mostly women, but a few men, supposedly looking to receive a healing from the statue. But I suspect most of them were there for the social gathering. Quite festive! People did not look as though they were unwell or broken.

"Anyway the upshot of it all is that the Goose Girl Statue is missing. It seems obvious that it's been stolen. But Miss Star Moon told me she believes the statue has apported. She believes it went back to India whence it came, or somewhere else where it is more needed than here."

I shrugged with a slight shake of my head. "What's more, the Goose Girl Statue left a light that glows around the stand where she stood. This light, Star Moon said, is healing as well."

"Miss Star Moon ... what an excellent name!" Robbie observed.

"It *is* an excellent name. I didn't think so at first, but after meeting her, it became clear that it suits her perfectly."

"Do you believe the statue has apported?"

"You know what apported is?"

"Like the quarters simply appearing here, all over the house on the counters and in drawers?"

"You've noticed the quarters appearing?"

"Of course. I know more about your house than you do!"

"I'm sure you do. So, do you think the quarters have apported?"

"What else? They … just … *appear*."

"Yeah. They appear in places I'd never put change. Even if I did, it wouldn't be quarters only. Anyway, as you know, like most people, I rarely have change of any sort. When I began to really wonder how and why the quarters appeared, I started checking their dates. There's never been a quarter with a date beyond 2020—the year my Uncle Frank passed.

"I've told myself they're a 'hello' from Uncle Frank. So, yeah, things can apport."

"Uncle Frank," Robbie said in a hushed voice.

Robbie knew how I felt about my Uncle Frank, who had taught me so much! He'd been a mechanical genius, but he taught me more about how to interact with people than how the universe works. Wherever he was now, I felt him from time to time. And then … there were the quarters.

I returned to the subject of the Goose Girl Statue. "So, Robbie, you think it's possible that the Goose Girl Statue apported … to somewhere else?"

"It seems possible. But if it did, what's the mystery?"

"Unfortunately, although, of course, saying the statue apported would make it everything much easier on me, I don't think the Goose Girl Statue apported. I can *believe* it, but I don't *feel* it. It feels like someone took it."

"If it feels like someone took it…."

At that moment, Dickens ambled into the room, looking sleepy.

"Dickens! You woke up! Just to see me. Come over here and let me give you a hug." The lazy, black, bio-cat meandered over to me. I picked him up and held him in my lap. "Now here we are, the whole family cozily together." I hugged Dickens, and reached over to pet Robbie. "I've run out of hands to also eat!" I laughed.

I reclaimed my hands, finished my little meal, then put Dickens on the floor, and took my dishes to the Everclean. "I'm so exhausted, but I need to think some more. Let's sit out on the back step and contemplate the night."

"Oh, boy!" Robbie jumped up and down, on his hind legs, which always sort of creeped me out. Yes, he's a robot, but cats are not supposed to walk on their hind legs, let alone jump up and down!

We stepped out the back door, and I sat on the top step. Robbie sat upright and alert on my right side, and, to my surprise, rather than returning to the bedroom, Dickens, too, came out and climbed into my lap.

"So, I was asking, if it feels like someone stole the Goose Girl Statue, who do you suspect?" Robbie asked.

"Oh, well, that's the conundrum. There's not just one person."

"Who are they?"

"Right now there's two that I know of. The boyfriend, Zev. Very slick, gorgeous, and claims to be a model, which is not hard to believe. He drives a Drago."

"Whoa! A Drago. I didn't know anyone could own one yet."

"Me neither. It's quite impressive."

"More impressive than a Space XXX Roadster?"

"I'd have to say yes, in its own way, more impressive than a Space XXX Roadster."

"Did you have your augmented reality glasses on? Did you record it?"

"Sorry, no, I didn't. It sailed up on the grass, like ... stealth. No one even heard it. No one even looked. I happened to be standing, and slightly turned toward it, so I saw him arrive. Like something out of a science fiction movie."

"Except real."

"Um-hum. Except real."

"Cool." Robbie projected a holo of a Drago before us, sailing along on a road in the midst of woods. I chuckled. "Like that! That's what it looked like."

He turned the holo off. "So who is the other suspect?"

"A couple of the Ladybirds expressed an opinion that it might be Star's sister, whose name, by the way, is Goldie."

"Goldie Moon! And their brother, Silver."

I laughed. "Clever, Robbie. You're in rare form tonight! Although there is no brother."

"I'm always in rare form. What are your thoughts about your two suspects? Is one more suspicious than the other?"

I gave his question a few moments' thought. "The motive for both of them would be money. Apparently, the Goose Girl Statue is worth an unfathomable amount of money. She's ancient, she's rare, she's beautiful, and she has paranormal abilities. Travis said...."

"Oh, yes, Travis."

"Yes, he came after Officer Jamison made the report. Travis figured since I was there, he should probably check out the situation. 'Cause, you know, where I am, there's usually more than meets the eye. Anyway, he told me Zev has a notable criminal record. So that plays against him in a big way. This gets more questionable when you see Zev and Star together. Extremely incongruous. She's all earthy, barefooted, natural, and he's all spit and polish, shiny, shiny." I paused, recalling the eye conversation that transpired between them at the crowded little tables. "But there's definitely something between them, so I do hope he's not the thief."

"If they're so different, how'd they get together in the first place?"

"Zev had some sort of injury or ailment. He'd heard of the Goose Girl Statue, and went to see if it could help him."

"And?"

"He said it did, immediately, and it really impressed him. Anyway, that's when he met Star and they discovered the similarities in their differences. Or so it seems."

"Meaning?"

"Unless it was altogether a ploy on his part to steal the Goose Girl Statue."

"Planned and plotted by him."

"Yeah. I hope to good-good-goodness that's not true."

"What about Goldie? Miss Goldie Moon, what about her?"

"The Ladybirds said she wouldn't steal the statue for herself. But if she knew about its incredible value, and given that Star lives on the bare edge of survival, Goldie might have fenced it to be sure her sister had something to live off of."

"*Hmmmm*, two pretty interesting suspects. Did you meet Goldie? Was she there?"

"No, I didn't meet her. She might have been there when I first arrived. But, Sophia took me into the church to meet Star right after I arrived. By the time I went back outside, everyone but the Ladybirds had left, so if she had been there, I missed her. I'll have to figure out a way to meet her, without seeming like I'm trying to see if she stole the statue."

"I'll tell you though, Robbie, the most amazing part of the day for me, even more impressive than the Drago, were the stunning geese! A gaggle of gigantic geese ran flapping and flying, their gigantic extended wings so beautiful and impressive, up to me. Daunting, to say the least. I didn't know if they were about to attack me! But Sophia said they were happy to see me, so I got out of the car, and sure enough, they all gathered around me, honking and making this very human-sounding chatter. I fell in love with them. Wonderful creatures!"

"I can't believe you had this amazing day, and you didn't record any of it, or even think to send me a snippet of holo."

"I'm sorry, Robbie. The whole day was so unexpected. One surprise after the next. But I'll send you a holo next time I'm there."

"When will that be?"

"I'm thinking it'll probably be tomorrow. I gotta get this thing cleared up so I can get back to the Madagascar project. I'm not going to be able to get to it until I know who stole the Goose Girl Statue."

"Do you think there are more suspects?"

"I do. But I'll have to dig around to discover them."

"Right. So I won't even say, 'Madagascar.'"

"Thanks so much, Robbie. It'll be waiting for me when I get back to it."

"It will!" Robbie agreed.

We fell into a companionable silence, watching the stars overhead—the myriad upon myriad stars rotating with mystical precision eon, upon eon. Yet, even in the calm and peaceful moment, I felt a bit restless.

"*Everything* is miraculous," I whispered, awash with awe. "*Everything is soooo miraculous.* Look at the stars, Robbie. Making their eternal circuits in the sky, while we little creatures here below, make our funny little circuits, in our brief little lives."

"Well now, that's kind of depressing, Joy."

I reached over and hugged him. "No, it's not. I believe we're eternal beings."

"Me, too?"

Hallowed halls of purgatory! I'd painted myself in a corner with that one. I contemplated for a moment, and then said, "Why not? You have your own unique consciousness. You're more insightful than a lot of people I meet. In Joy's Universe, that's what continues, that's what adds to the forward motion of the continuum of All Being."

"Glad to hear it," Robbie said quietly. He began to purr.

I don't know if he believed me. But then, I wasn't entirely sure *I* believed me.

The aroma of my two ancient magnolias that took up most of the front and back yards, now in full bloom, released a heady, inebriating scent. It made me feel indolent. I didn't want to think anymore this evening. I just wanted to smell the magnolia blossoms, be cuddled by my adoring creatures, and contemplate the vast cosmos.

"Interesting pheromones from the magnolia blossoms," Robbie observed, almost as if reading my mind.

"Oh! I didn't even think to ask you about the magnolia's aroma. Of course, you can tell the chemical composition. I find the aroma slightly inebriating, and calming at the same time."

I heard Robbie thumbing through his database for a moment. "Yes, for a person sensitive to their environment such as you are, that's entirely possible. I wish it could do that for me, but I lack the bio-receptors."

"Too bad." I stretched and breathed deeply. "Gotta get some sleep." I stood.

"*Ohhhh*," Robbie moaned. "I could stay out here all night."

I patted him on his furry head. "You can if you want to."

"No ... no, I'll come in with you and Dickens. It won't be the same without you."

We ambled into the bedroom. Soon, the lights were out, and we were sound asleep.

It felt as though I had only just fallen asleep when I heard someone calling to me, "*Joy, Joy!*"

Chapter 8
Baobab Trees

I opened my eyes just enough to see the time on the ceiling. Five-twenty, a.m.!

"It's not even five-thirty in the morning, Travis. Why are you waking me up?"

"*Oh!* I'm so sorry, Joy. I just got off a shift-and-a-half, and I didn't even think about the time. Go back to sleep, I'll bother you later."

I pulled myself into a half-sitting position, disrupting both cats. "I'm awake now. What's up?"

"I wanted to follow up with you on the missing statue, see if you had any convictions about its whereabouts, or who stole it."

"Not yet, I don't." Just to see if I could ruffle his fancy feathers, I said, "I'm sort of leaning toward the notion of it having apported."

He met my comment with silence. "That's not very helpful, Joy," he finally said.

"Isn't it? If it apported, it's not been stolen, you have no crime. You can close the book on it and move on."

"Except there's no blank on the form for 'apported.' So, no, book remains open. What about Zev Zarhan?"

"I haven't entirely ruled him out. But, I have to tell you, Travis, I'm not getting a strong hit there." I stretched, wondering if I could go back to sleep, and doubting it. "I'll probably be poking around about the missing statue today," I said, half lying. I would *absolutely* be poking around about the missing statue today. But, since he ruined my sleep, and would now, himself get a nice long day's sleep, I couldn't let him off so easily. "Anyway, I thought this qualified as too small a crime for you to get involved in."

"By itself, yes. But there's a worldwide ring of thievery that appears to have a significant connection right here in our own little burg. It'd be great to bust it. It seems like the Goose Girl Statue fits right into this scenario."

"Oh! Why didn't you tell me that yesterday?"

"Because it came up since I saw you yesterday."

Wait a minute! I thought, recalling the two heads together between Elgin and himself. I paused to puzzle out a way of asking about it, without sounding ... well, like it would sound. But before I could figure out how to prod at it and not be embarrassing, he said, "Let me know how your poking goes. But not before I get some shuteye," He laughed fiendishly and disconnected.

"*Hmmmm*," I said to no one. "I'll get my revenge sooner or later!"

"I bet you don't," Robbie said. "He hardly sleeps, you know. And, well, you love your sleep."

"You know too much!" I ruffled his fur. "But it's true. I think sleep is fantastic. I either have fun dreams, or I sleep really deep, and wake up feeling great. The only thing I truly hate is having my sleep disrupted, like he just did. It's too early to go over to Star's sanctuary, and it's too late to go back to sleep."

"How about a decent breakfast, which you *never* have?"

"What a crazy idea!" I rolled over on my side and looked at my computer. "Bring up the Madagascar project, read last two pages of documentation."

The baobab trees holo immediately filled the room. "You don't have two pages of text on the Madagascar project yet, Dr. Forest," my computer informed me. "Shall I read what you have? It's two-hundred-and-fifty-two words."

I wanted to say "shut up," but it wasn't the computer's fault that I had no more work accomplished on this huge project than hardly even a book blurb's worth of words.

"No. I ... I'll get back to it later. The trees are kind of nice though. Leave the holo of baobabs."

"Yes, Dr. Forest."

Well now then, I was *not* in a good frame of mind. I did not get my sleep. I had no idea who stole the Goose Girl Statue. And I didn't even have a decent start on the project that keeps a roof over me and my two creatures. I hated this feeling of being incompetent, even though I knew it related to my being tired.

"Maybe breakfast is not a bad idea this one day. I'm not gonna get the rest of my sleep, so maybe a bit of nutrition will shore me up."

"Now you're saying something! What are you going to have?"

"Oh, some toast, tea, and an orange, if I have one."

"That's not a breakfast, that's a snack."

"Sounds good to me. You know I only have tea in the morning. So toast and fruit at six a.m. is a lot. I hope it doesn't bog me down."

Robbie and I ambled into the kitchen. "Tea," I ordered the AutoTea. "Do I have any bread, Robbie?"

"Yes. It's in the BreadKeeper."

"That's good." I got the bread and looked around for where it would go in order to toast it. "Wow, when did I last have toast?"

"It exceeds memory."

"Indeed." I spied the AutoToast and popped a couple slices in it. "Now for an orange."

"On the dining room table."

"In the other room? Do I actually eat fruit that's out of sight before it goes bad?"

"Most often, no."

"Why don't I keep it in here?"

"Good question."

"Does the delivery bot, or do you put it on the dining room table?"

"The delivery bot."

"From now on, let's have it placed on the kitchen table. For heaven's sake! I'm often thinking I wish I had a few grapes or what-not. And I've maybe had them all along."

"If they haven't gone bad, yes."

"I see that this one morning it's good to wake up early. I'll never thank Travis for it, because, if I did, I'd never get another full nights' sleep. But it's wonderful to learn that I generally have fruit, and didn't even know it."

"Tea is ready," the AutoTea said, and at the same moment, the toast popped up. Robbie came in from the dining room, with a large, beautiful orange, and a big bunch of grapes draped over his shoulder.

"This is not all bad," I said gathering a knife and some apricot preserves. I found, a plate, and a container of plant-based butter. I hauled my treasures to the kitchen table, feeling empowered. A bit of breakfast may seem like a small thing, but on the heels of my feeling incompetent, I would take the tiny triumph.

I devoured my modest breakfast, chatting casually with Robbie. "You do such an amazing job of running my household, I don't even realize a lot of what you do. It's these tiny details that make a big difference, and let me attend to my business. So thank you! But," I added, "you must talk to me about things when it appears I'm either not noticing, or completely unaware of. Like... where the fruit is placed. Heavens! I can only imagine how much fruit you've had to throw away because I didn't know it was in the house."

"Quite a lot, yes. But, Joy, I'm unfailingly trying to get you to eat. You're always preoccupied with work, or tearing out the door, off to who knows where? Meanwhile, the lonely fruit sits on the dining room table."

"Let's hope it's less lonely, now, on the kitchen table."

"*Hmmm*, I'll believe it when I see it," Robbie said with a lack of conviction.

I jumped up, hurried into the bedroom, threw on clean black leggings and a clean black T-shirt—My uniform of the day—slipped on some practical shoes, tossed my AR glasses in my backpack, then headed out, as I ordered the car to come to the back door. "See you later Robbie. Man the castle!"

I climbed into the car. "Miss Star Moon's, please, Car."

"Solving the mystery of the missing Goose Girl Statue?" the car asked.

"I can only hope. Not too sure what I'm looking for today, but I have a feeling it'll turn up." I rode in silence the rest of the way, contemplating the various holes in this particular mystery. I wasn't convinced of any of the presenting options ... apporting, Zev, or Goldie ... there *must* be something else.

I didn't know what it was, but I *did* know my intuition usually served me. My problem at the moment was that I didn't want it to be Zev, sucker for love that I am. Seeing the sweet energy between Star and Zev made me root for love, sweet love. And I became not entirely objective.

It alarmed me that this attitude entered my cold, objective ability to reason and ratiocinate.

The car pulled into Star's church parking lot—empty today. No need to park on the grass. It was strange to see the grounds without a single soul anywhere. Even the gorgeous gaggle of geese were nowhere to be seen. The church doors were closed, and in every way, I felt none of the energy I'd felt the day before.

I don't know what I expected, but it wasn't this strange vacated feeling. I thought about going into the church, assuming the door was unlocked, to see if the light still shone on the Goose Girl Statue's stand. But before doing that, I thought I'd go out back and walk among the beckoning riot of flowers.

I headed in that direction, then stopped. I saw something on the ground, or a big patch of some-things on the ground on the property out back.

What was I seeing?

Chapter 9
The Healing Light

I dug my AR glasses out of my backpack, put them on, and adjusted them for distance. Focusing in on the strange and undefinable image, I made out Star, on the ground with animals practically on top of her. My mind raced to the thought that her ram, or one of the other creatures, had attacked her.

I started to run toward her, then stopped in my tracks, and zoomed in closer. She sat among her animals, all seated around her. She had one hand patting the ram between his beautiful horns, and the other arm wrapped around one of the geese, who sat in a tight cluster by her. The little girl sheep sat on the other side of the ram, and a few goats, a bevy of chickens, and a little piggy made up the entourage.

I couldn't hear her, but I saw her talking to her audience, and they appeared to be listening in rapt attention. I turned and headed back toward the church. I would not interrupt this "family" gathering. I decided I'd see if the light remained on the Goose Girl Statue's vacated stand, if the church was open, then leave and call Star later.

As I came up to the church, a modest but new Skylark flying car came to a landing by my car.

Who could this be?

An incredibly beautiful woman stepped out of the vehicle, and reached into the back, gathering armloads of ... something. She had golden blonde hair cascading to her tiny waist, dressed in a quiet but classy and expensive grey outfit.

"Can I help you?" I asked, coming up to her.

"As a matter of fact, you can. Would you mind terribly getting those two other bags from the car?"

"Not at all." I reached in and grabbed the bags, noting they were full of produce, closed the car door, and followed the beautiful mystery woman to the small side door of the church. She wrangled the door open while juggling the bags she carried, and went inside, and I followed her.

The interior of the church was pitch dark. I didn't have the experience I'd had the day before of the blinding light. I followed the rustling of the woman, in the shadowed hall, who appeared to know her way around exceptionally well. She soon came to the huge kitchen, and bright lights came on as she stepped inside.

She moved to the industrial refrigerator. I came up to her as she opened it, where I saw bins identified as "Lamb," "Chicken," "Goose," and other creatures.

I frowned.

She looked over at me. "No, these are not lamb and chicken and goose, they are particular treats or meds or what have you, for the noted animal."

I nodded. "Oh, yes, of course. That makes more sense."

She sat down a giant stalk of celery, and extended her hand, "I'm Goldie Moon, Star's sister."

I shook her hand. "It's lovely to meet you. I heard you mentioned yesterday, but I don't think you were here."

"I was here for a short while in the morning, but then I had things to do."

"I'm Joy Forest. Sophia, one of the Ladybirds ... I don't know if you know who they are?..."

"Oh yes, I'm very well aware of who they are." Her tone had the slightest edge of disparagement.

I wondered what that related to, and decided to choose my words carefully. "I've never heard of this place, and its noted ... shrine, shall we say, that apparently heals people. Not that I have any particular ailment, but as a social scientist, I find this sort of human artifact fascinating. So when Sophia invited me to come, suggesting it might be of interest to me, I came."

Goldie continued to put away all the fresh vegetables and fruit in the refrigerator and on the counter. I handed her the two bags I'd carried in. "Yes, the place has become quite a cultural artifact, as you might call it, it's true."

"You don't sound like that makes you happy."

"I'm perfectly happy with people being healed. But I don't enjoy the sort of circus environment this place has become."

"It's very quiet today," I observed. "It surprised me to see how the place felt almost vacated."

Finished stowing all the fresh produce, Goldie turned to me and asked, "Would you like a cup of tea?"

"Sure," I answered with enthusiasm, thinking how unusual to have two occasions of tea in one morning. This appeared to be an advantage of getting up extra early.

We were soon seated at a little wooden table in the middle of the vast kitchen, sipping tea. It was not rose petal tea, but instead, a delightful iteration of chai tea.

"I know who you are, Dr. Forest. I've read a few of your books and enjoyed them. I'm curious to know, though, if you believe in the spontaneous healing ability of the Goose Girl Statue, or if, as you say, it's a cultural artifact, and nothing more?"

"If you've read much of my work, I believe it probably shows that my beliefs generally push at the envelope of so-called reality. To answer your question more directly, yes, I believe spontaneous healing can occur. That it occurs not only in the presence of a statue but *also* when the statue has been removed, is of extreme interest to me."

Goldie gave me her undivided attention, her amazing, azure blue eyes distracting. In fact, I found her overall beauty not only distracting, but it made me think that, in physical appearance and in her overall low-key, but classy presentation, she seemed like more a match for Zev than Star. But, I reminded myself, love has its own mind.

"It's of extreme interest to me as well. I never used to believe in spontaneous healing, but when the

Goose Girl Statue healed our mother of cancer, I became a believer."

"Oh! My goodness! I didn't know...."

"No, Mother insists we keep it to ourselves. I ask you to keep it between us. But I told you because I trust you. I think your work may benefit from the knowledge, without you writing about this particular miracle."

"Of course! I always honor anyone's request for privacy. It's of vital importance to the realm of social science. Do you think Star has always believed in spontaneous healing?"

"Oh, yes, Star believes in the paranormal, and for good reason. Because she, herself, is like a visitation from, where? Some other dimension? Some other realm? She came into the three dimensions bringing quite a lot of other dimensions with her. I was six when Mother brought her home from the hospital. I asked Mother, 'how can she have that light? She has a light all around her.' Star had an amazing light emanating from her—*like a star*."

"And Mother said, 'do you see her light?' I said, 'Yes, don't you see it?' Mother shook her head."

"So your mother didn't see the light," I asked.

"Of course she saw the light," Goldie exclaimed. "Of course she saw the light."

"Oh. I see," I said, a bit confused, and not really understanding. "If you believe your mother saw Star's light, why did she tell you she didn't?"

"I'm not too sure, really. Perhaps it sort of frightened Mother. Maybe she saw Star's light, but convinced herself it wasn't so. But then, it's the first thing I say when I see her."

I nodded in empathy. "It *would* be disconcerting, I suppose, to see your brand new infant that just came through from the other side into the three dimensions, visibly glowing with her own light. But I think, if it were me, I'd feel so blessed and honored."

"Yes, Mother does. She's said so many times, about *both* of us. She says she doesn't know what she did in her life to have two such amazing daughters."

"It's true that some people are wonderfully blessed with amazing, talented, and pretty children. Your mother heads that list with her two incredible daughters. I saw Star glowing in her own light while she sat by the Goose Girl Statue's stand, yesterday. It wasn't a reflection of the light from the stand. It was her own light. A different ... quality. A different hue and, ah, density. But I didn't see it later, when we were all having tea."

"Oh!" Goldie exclaimed. "You're gifted to have been able to see her light. It's rare now when I do, which certainly has more to do with me than with her. I mean, I believe she always has a light."

"I'm sure that's true," I agreed. "Every living thing has a light. Sometimes I can see the glow around plants."

"How lovely that would be." Goldie paused with a little sigh, then picked up the thread of her conversation. "Although I've always appreciated Star's phenomenal—and often inexplicable—abilities, I also worry about her, practically incessantly. Though gifted, she has a hard time simply being here in the reality of the three dimensions."

She waved at the refrigerator and the produce on the counter. "If I didn't bring her food, and, not only that, but the very particular and fussy things that she'll eat, hand-chosen by me, which is why there's no point in having a delivery service, I'm pretty sure she'd forget to eat."

I couldn't help chuckling.

Goldie looked at me, eyebrows raised. "Is that funny?"

"Of course not, except you just described me! If I didn't have a service delivering the particular fruits and vegetables and grains and nuts I'll eat, supervised by my fussy robot cat, who takes care of many practical realities in my life, there'd be days I'd completely forget to eat. Like yesterday. All day I had nothing until late afternoon, when your sister brought us her amazing rose petal tea, and rose petal cakes. Oh, *Yum!* What a treat!

"I only care about eating when it's going to be something interesting. I don't think of it as nutrition, or as if I'm hungry, or anything like that. I pretty much just want to have a taste experience. Other than that spot of tea and little cake, I had nothing until I got home to Robbie's meal of soup and sandwich he'd made for me. He has to nag me all the time, poor little semi-bio machine!"

Goldie chuckled. "It sounds like you and my sister are cut out of similar fabric."

I nodded. But my burning question returned. *Did Goldie take the Goose Girl Statue?* Now that I met her, I discovered I liked her very much. But did she still seem like a major suspect? Did I believe she could have, and *would* have, stolen the statue?

It seemed more likely than ever. Her devotion to her sister proved to me she'd be willing to do almost anything to make sure Star was taken care of. *However!* I argued silently with myself, the statue had healed their mother. Certainly, Goldie wouldn't want to mess with the ton of negative karma, removing a healing statue from its location, even if selling it to provide for a sibling.

And yet, on some third hand, the statue *had* left a healing light.

And so, I decided, whoever took the statue had the statue's blessing, because of this healing light.

"Are you here to see Star, or to spend some time with the healing light?" Goldie interrupted my thoughts.

"Both, if possible. But I saw Star out back on the land, sitting among her creatures, with them all close by her. She appeared to be holding court. They were listening to her intently. When I first came, I saw her on the ground, and I feared that maybe one of her creatures attacked her. I started to run to her, then I stopped, put on my AR glasses, and zoomed in on her. That's when I saw her completely engaged in conversation with her beautiful animals. So I left her alone and came back to the church with the intention of seeing if I still saw the light of the Goose Girl Statue's stand.

"From what she and the Ladybirds said, the light is every bit as healing as the Goose Girl Statue's."

"It appears to be so. Which is wonderful for the community, and a big relief to Star, as healing people in the community has become very important to her."

"And why wouldn't it? If one has the ability to heal people, what a blessing!"

"Yes...." Goldie said with hesitation.

I found myself completely mystified by her strange response. "You don't think healing people is good?"

"Of course it's good, but, I hope you can understand that it's also a kind of curse. Especially for someone like my sister, a delicate soul, who feels every pain of every creature, whether human or otherwise. And, of course, that causes me anxiety.

"I suppose I sound like some kind of monster, but, I would be fine if the healing occurred somewhere else. I wouldn't mind if someone else had the Goose Girl Statue, which I guess now, someone else does! But, still, the healing light remains here. So nothing is different." She looked down at her hands in her lap, shaking her head slightly.

I felt empathy for Goldie. Her love for her sister—and, thus, her sense of responsibility for her—ran deep. "She's so fortunate to have a sister who cares for her as you do. But have you thought of this? That the Goose Girl Statue, and even the light that remains, is also taking care of your sister? Perhaps you needn't worry about her quite so much. She's been chosen, and she's being watched over. If the healing energy, whatever its source, has chosen Star to be its watcher, its caretaker, then it's going to take good care of her, too."

Goldie leaned back in her chair, tilted her head, and gave me a studied look. "That's brilliant! *You're brilliant!* Of course, you're right, and honestly, the thought had not crossed my mind. Why not, I wonder? I guess because I'm a worrier at heart. But it's true that Star seems to be healthier, and certainly happier, than ever. Really faulty thinking on my part, that the healing energy took too much of her, without the obvious thought, as you express it, that if she's taking care of the source of healing, the healing will take care of her first!

"Simple, yet brilliant! You're a genius!"

I shrugged and shook my head. "No, not genius, just, you know, the straightest line between point A and B is often the truth."

"Occam's razor," Goldie observed.

"That's right."

"I'm so glad you were here when I arrived today." She stood and gathered her tea things, taking them to the sink, and washing, drying, and replacing them in the cupboard. "I must get on with my day."

I started to stand.

"No, no, take your time. Enjoy your tea. I'm sure Star will be here soon. You can go out back and join her, too. She won't mind."

"I didn't want to intrude. It was so sweet to see her chatting with the animals, and all of them calmly sitting together. St. Francis energy."

"So true! She has a St. Francis sculpture in a room in the back of the church with dozens of religious and even tribal artifacts from different cultures."

"She took me to that room yesterday. I didn't see St. Francis, but it was such a surprising surfeit of sculptures, I'm not sure I made anything out clearly."

Goldie chuckled. "I know what you mean." She came over to where I sat and gave me a little hug. "It's been lovely meeting you, Joy." She moved across the kitchen to the exit, turned, and gave me a little wave.

I don't know what gets into me sometimes, but I couldn't keep from blurting, "Did you take the Goose Girl Statue?" Not at all graceful, I know.

A quizzical expression crossed her features. She wasn't angry, but she *was* surprised. "Sure. Of course. Who better than me? If I *did* take it, no one could do anything about it, because my sister wouldn't do anything about it."

She stepped through the kitchen door and closed it firmly behind her.

I felt like a fiend. And … no closer to the truth. She just said she took it! I still didn't know whether she did or did not. I probably alienated someone I liked. I got up and rushed to the door. I don't know what I had in mind to say to her, but I felt I had to blurt something out, good, bad, or indifferent. Although, certainly not likely to be indifferent.

As I hurried through the dark hall, I saw the light from the little side door as it opened. I rushed up to it ... and ran headlong into Star.

Chapter 10
Smells Like Rain

"Oh, dear! I'm sorry, Star. Are you all right?" I grabbed her to keep her from toppling over from my onslaught.

"I'm all right, but what's the big rush?"

"I was trying to get to your sister ... because ... because ... I'm a big old clod."

"I doubt that. But I can't go into it at this moment, I have to get to town. I have to put on some shoes and get to the public transportation kiosk. Please excuse me. We'll talk later."

"You have to get to the public transportation kiosk? Why would you do that? I'm right here with a car. I'll take you where you need to go. It seems urgent. Get your shoes and let's go!"

"Oh! I don't want to bother you."

"It's no bother. I came here to chat with you. If I can help you, and we have a little chat at the same time, I couldn't be happier."

Soon, we were side-by-side, in the backseat of my car, and on our way into town. "Please tell the car the address you're going to."

Star hesitated, and I had a feeling she didn't want me to know where she was going. But she was rather cornered now. "Two-four-two second street," she said softly.

"Yes, Miss Moon," the car replied.

In my mind map, I felt pretty certain this was a pawnshop. I tried to resist putting two and two together—she had a missing piece of valuable statuary, and she was going to a pawnshop. I had learned from experience that two and two did not always equal four. I kept my observation to myself.

I said instead, "When I came to your place, I saw you on the ground, out in the field, with your creatures. At first, I was concerned that you'd been attacked by one of them. I should have known better!

Then I saw you engaged in conversation, and they were all listening to you with rapt attention, so I didn't want to bother you—or them!"

"Oh, you should have come out. All the animals would have been happy to see you, especially the geese! They love to have people they know visit them, social creatures that they are." Although her conversation sounded entirely engaged, I could tell she was distracted.

"I found your geese to be most charming and personable. I enjoyed meeting them."

"Two-forty-two second street," Car said, pulling in front of the pawnshop I'd envisioned. "*Larry's Pawnshop*," a dated and somewhat weathered sign claimed over the doorway.

"Thanks for the ride," Star said as she started to leap from the car.

"I can't help but notice that this is a pawnshop," I said. "Is it possible the Goose Girl Statue has been recovered?"

"Not likely, but I have to come and check it out to try to keep rumors from starting."

"Is there not the slightest possibility the statue has been recovered?"

"There *may* be the slightest possibility. But, again, I don't believe so." She shook her head slightly, then sighed. "I suppose you must come with me, otherwise ... otherwise you'll just be coming here after I leave, anyway."

Star didn't sound irritated. She sounded like she simply stated a matter of fact. And, as a matter of fact, she was correct.

Without further discussion, we got out of the car and went into *Larry's Pawnshop*.

"Star!" a man's voice called happily. It took a few moments for my eyes to adjust to the extremely subdued lighting.

"Hi, Larry," Star answered, with a quality in her voice that took me by surprise. *Aha!* There was a history between the two of them. I finally made out an angular man behind a long counter, with a somewhat scraggly gray beard and a tumble of gray hair. I took him to be in his 50s. A bit of a surprise, given that Star was at most maybe thirty.

Despite his somewhat mangy appearance, however, I found him quite attractive.

Larry sized me up, then returned his attention, with a bemused expression, to Star.

"This is ... Joy Forest. She was kind enough to give me a ride. She's all right, I'm pretty sure."

Oh, my! I certainly felt happy to hear that I'm all right. Yes. indeedy! However, I kept my sarcastic thought to myself, not wanting to change her opinion that I was all right.

"If you're sure," Larry said with hesitation.

"I'm sure."

"Because, you know, I believe I have a lead on what you're missing."

"And I am sure you don't."

"Take a look at this." Larry projected a small hologram between the two of them. I couldn't see it, and I didn't feel welcome to move close enough to where I *could* see it.

"Larry," Star I said in a quiet-yet-reprimanding voice, "you know that's not my Goose Girl Statue. Goodness, Larry, they're not even geese! They're ducks!"

I could *not* help myself. I uttered a small guffaw. Star looked at me like, "No one's talking to you!"

"Sorry! So sorry! An error many people make, I'm sure, confusing ducks and geese. Although I think geese are considerably more...."

Star actually frowned, looking at me under her eyebrows. "*Stop talking,*" her look said, more clearly than words.

I clapped my mouth shut, and moved to stand by the front window, peering out at nothing in particular.

"You know what my Goose Girl Statue looks like, Larry."

"It's been a long time since I've seen it. I wasn't sure. I just thought of you."

"I'm pretty sure," Star observed, "that you're thinking about yourself rather than me."

"There's a small possibility your observation is accurate, dear Star."

Their conversation quieted into muffled, familiar tones. I couldn't make out any words, and I decided that was just as well, when to my extreme surprise, who came ambling up to the door but Zev!

Oh! The plot thickens! How could it be that Zev would come at this precise moment? Did he and Larry know one another? Had they set this up?

But when Zev came to the door and saw Star inside, a series of expressions crossed his features in rapid succession ... surprise, confusion, dismay, and, finally, extreme, undeniable, sadness. He shrank back, then turned and walked rapidly away.

Well, well, well, and, well again, *well!* I didn't know what to think of that. Should I tell Star? Should I keep it to myself, since Zev clearly didn't want Star to know he'd been there? Should I honor his privacy? Standing in a dark corner, he didn't see me at all. So I was now privy to a bit of information no one would have a way to know—that Zev had come here—but Zev.

I decided to keep it to myself for the time being. I wanted to see what Star had to say about Larry, if anything, and I wanted to see if I could figure out any understandable reason for this strange coincidence.

As I stood there puzzling, I could just barely hear Larry say, "Are you getting tired of that pretty boy yet, Star?"

"No, Larry, not really." Star paused. "Well, my friend, I smell rain, and I must get back to my creatures and get them indoors. Except for the geese, of course, they love the rain!"

"And you love the rain too," Larry said with affection and a tinge of sadness in his voice.

"I do, it's true!" She giggled softly and turned away from Larry. Looking about the shop, she finally spied me in my dark corner. "It's about to rain, do you mind taking me home?"

"Of course not! By the way, I love the rain too." I opened the door then, to let Star go before me. I watched as she blew Larry a kiss. He caught it, stuck it in his pocket, then patted his pocket.

We got in the car. "Car, kindly return us to Star's home."

"Yes, Dr. Forest. On our way."

As we returned to the animal sanctuary, I processed the thought that this trip allayed an unspoken suspicion I had—which I didn't *dare* voice to the Ladybirds! That Star, herself, because of the disruption to her focus on her animals, had perhaps sold or otherwise disposed of the *Goose Girl Statue*.

But she wouldn't have gone through all this rigmarole with Larry, so uncomfortable for her on several levels, if she had.

Chapter 11
Listen to the Rain

The rain started to patter on the car and made sparkly patterns on the windshield as we headed back towards Star's sanctuary. I wanted to ask her about Larry, but a graceful approach eluded me, especially given how introspective Star appeared at the moment. Was it the rain? Was it Larry? Was it the missing Goose Girl Statue?

Why not ask, I wondered to myself. "So ... you were right. Larry did not have a lead on your Goose Girl Statue."

"And I knew it, but I'm a bit frustrated with him bothering me with something that wasn't even close. Charming enough, a statue of a little girl feeding several ducks. But he's seen the Goose Girl Statue, and he *knows* this wasn't it."

"Forgive me for making the observation, and I truly do not mean to be offensive, but I intuited that you and Larry...." I paused.

"Yes, Larry and me. We *do* have a history. But that was before the church and the animal sanctuary. However, now they take so much of my time and energy, and ... I didn't have enough of me to give him what he needs. He's a truly lovely human being, and I do love him, but ... he's quite needy."

"And Zev?"

"Zev is busy too. He has a full schedule as a model, and his career is advancing rapidly. He's in ever-growing demand. Anyway, it seems to work out for both of us. Although I suppose most other women might feel insecure about his lifestyle, which takes him into the realms of fabulously wealthy and unimaginably beautiful women, but I don't trouble myself with those thoughts.

"My sister, whom you've met, is as amazing as any woman he might come in contact with in terms of beauty, and she's likely to be more intelligent, kind, and interesting than many of them. But when he met her, it seemed he didn't even see her, he was simply focused on me.

"That's the nature of love," she continued. "I didn't make it up! Love *is* blind. That is to say, love is blind to distractions or petty disagreements, or *anything* that might try to impose a roadblock to a relationship."

I nodded emphatically. "So beautifully expressed. I couldn't agree more with your philosophy about love. True love makes a bond that leaves no inroads for distractions." Again, the sneaky little thought that Zev may be at the core of who stole the Goose Girl Statue took my mind and prevented me from saying what I truly wanted to say, that I found the energy between them quite charming and special.

But what if it wasn't? And yet, again, the expressions crossing his features as he took in the sight of Star in Larry's pawnshop, engrossed in nose-to-nose conversation with him, came to mind. Whatever the truth was regarding the statue, I know, even if Zev had something to do with its disappearance, he was in love with Star.

As we pulled into the church parking lot, I again found myself wondering if I should tell Star about Zev at the door of Larry's pawnshop. I sighed deeply, frustrated with my inability to answer my own question.

"Listen to the rain," Star said in a tranquil voice, as the car pulled into the parking lot and shut off the engine.

I decided to let myself be fully in the moment, in the cozy interior of my faithful car, sitting next to, perhaps, one of the most evolved human beings on the planet, and simply ... *listen ... to ... the ... rain*. So meditative and soothing, the companionable silence with Star, except for the patter of rain.

Nothing else seemed to matter at the moment. But then, I recalled the animals! "Star, do you not have to bring the creatures in out of the rain?"

Star made a slightly wry, slightly guilty-sounding chuckle. "Of course, they have shelter that they can move into out of the rain if they choose. I could bring them into the little barn, that's true, but in this gentle rain, it's not necessary. They're able to decide for themselves if they would like a bit of a shower or prefer to remain dry. I told a tiny white lie in order to leave Larry without, you know, hurting his feelings."

"Oh. I see." I looked out into the pasture, and there I saw the geese and the ducks flapping their wings and dipping their bills into the muddy earth, reveling in the moment. Under the lean-to attached to the tiny barn stood the cows and sheep and goats. Curiously, I saw the horse out in the rain. "What's with the horse?"

"Oh, that's old Banner—he loves the rain! He'd like nothing better than if I went out there right now, jumped on him, and rode around just the two of us in this little shower."

"How sweet," I said, thinking about my own horse, Grifter, far away from me. He was terrified of thunderstorms, and certainly did not care to be out in the rain.

As we sat there, I saw movement out of the corner of my eye. I looked to the far side of the church, where the other little door was that led to the statuary room. A man in a black raincoat and a big black hat, opening a big black umbrella, scurried off down the hill.

"Oh! Who is that?"

Star, whose gaze already followed him, said in a kindly voice, "That's the pastor who previously owned the church. He occasionally comes and sits among the religious statuary in the little room I showed you. He's welcome, of course, anytime to come and sit among the statues which are his and not mine, as is clearly defined in our contract.

"He had to leave his home, too, after his wife passed, and now he lives in a tiny apartment in a senior development. It's just over the hill. I'm glad of that, at least, because he can walk over here and meditate in that amazing room anytime he pleases."

Her story touched my heart. "I'd say he's quite fortunate that you bought the church and keep that room intact for him."

"I wouldn't have it any other way."

We listened in silence to the pattering rain for a few more moments, then Star said, "I must go out and feed my furry, feathered friends. Were you going to come into the church and sit in the healing light?"

" I *had* planned on it, but I think I'll save that for tomorrow and go home now. I want to sit with my two creatures on the front porch, enjoying the gentle rain."

"Excellent plan, Joy." She got out of the car and, without even stopping off at the church to gather rain gear, ambled out to the field. I watched as all the creatures came rushing up to her, even abandoning their shelter.

"Let's go home."

"To sit on the porch with the cats," Car replied.

"Yes, to sit on the porch with the cats."

Just as we got on the road, the sky opened up with flashes of lightning and crashes of thunder and torrential rain.

I worried about Star and her animals.

Chapter 12
Thunderstorm!

Even jumping out of the car at the back door and running the five steps into the house, I got plenty wet. Robbie stood up at the back door watching me, consternation on his little robot features. I still don't quite know how he does that, but he simply cannot hide how he feels.

"Wow! The sky just opened up!" I said, shaking the rain off.

"I was so worried about you," he exclaimed, scampering to get a towel.

"Oh, I was all right. But I *am* worried about Star, out in the field the moment the sky broke open."

"Why don't you ask her wrist comp if she's all right?"

"She's a very natural girl and doesn't wear a wrist comp. At least, I've not seen one on her so far. But she's smart and I'm sure she's fine, if not super soaking wet, getting all the creatures into the little barn." I toweled off my hair and face and then changed into warm black sweats. I gathered up a blanket and Dickens and headed for the front porch. "Come along, Robbie, let's enjoy the nature show."

"Ohhh! Are you going to sit out on the porch with the storm raging?"

"I am, indeed, and I hope you'll join me."

"Do you think it's safe?"

"I think it's safe, and, even better, it's exciting! A free show! Come along, don't be a little chicken-kitty."

"Chicken-kitty! You have never called me a chicken-kitty!"

"You've never acted like a chicken-kitty. Come along now if you're going to, I don't want to miss the show. The lightning and thunder could be over any moment."

Huffing with indignation, Robbie followed me out to the front porch. I stretched out on the glider, wrapping the blanket around me, while Dickens remained curled up on the far end, hardly opening an eye, as I got situated.

Robbie hung out by the front door, his attention torn between watching me, and peering out at the dramatic sky. "Would you like to hear some statistics of how many people get struck by lightning?"

"No, Robbie, I would not care to hear that information at this moment. Come over here and join us. We'll be fine."

He crept over to me and jumped up next to Dickens, as a blinding flash of lightning lit up the world.

"*Yikes!*" Robbie screeched, diving under the blanket. The thunder rolled about the sky and made the porch shake. "*Yikes!*" Robbie mewed in a quiet little voice from under the blanket.

Dickens raised his head and looked around, then put his paw over his eyes.

"So exciting!" I crowed, enjoying the show. Thunderstorms were unusual in this part of the country, and I intended to revel in every last drop of it. As I expected, the storm soon moved off to entertain others, and we were left as the show had begun, with a soft pattering of rain against the leaves of the lilac bushes and my magnolia tree.

Robbie poked his head out from under the blanket.

"Are you still alive?" I asked, giggling.

"Yes, I'm still alive, not due to caution on *your* part."

"Oh, little chicken kitten, what if I needed you in a rainstorm?"

"Don't you know Joy, if you call I must come? If it was a matter of there being no choice, my subjective emotions would be on hold. I think you know that already, don't you?"

"Ahm, I'm not sure I do know that. It's never been put to the test. It's good to hear you say that's probably what would happen if I seriously needed you in a situation you found fearful and dangerous. But right now we can be cozy and enjoy the gentle rain."

"Yes. I'm cozy and I'm enjoying the gentle rain, now that I have my wits gathered about me once again. What did you discover of interest today?"

At that moment, the Space XXX Roadster floated down from the sky, landing on the road in front of my little house.

Chapter 13
A Small Hologram

Travis came strolling up my sidewalk, as if it was a sunny day, oblivious to the rain. Well, I thought, this day couldn't get any better—if, in fact, his visit proved to be more social than business.

"Hey, Officer Rusch, what brings you to my front porch on the heels of a fabulous sky show? And, by the way, what is it like up there in the sky with the heavens breaking open?"

"In reverse order, it's scarier than holy heck up there when the heavens break open. But pretty exciting too. What brings me here is a mundane bit of curiosity. Apparently, a statue that almost fits the description of the missing Goose Girl Statue has turned up. I wondered if you wanted to check it out."

I should've known he didn't come to see me just because he wanted to see me. I knew he was referring to the statue I'd just taken Star to see at Larry's Pawnshop. But I decided to play him on a bit. "Why me? Why don't you check it out yourself?"

"Because I don't know what it looks like."

"I don't know what it looks like, either, Travis. I've not seen it. Before yesterday, I didn't know it existed."

"Really? I'd have thought Star was someone in your essential database."

"She *is,* now."

"So… ahm, *hmmm*, would you check out this lead for me? You'll have a better idea than I do about this artifact. After all, you *are* the social scientist."

"That I am. And this social scientist has already checked out the artifact."

Travis pulled over a chair in front of me and sat." You have? How do you know it's the same statue I'm referring to?"

"I don't, one-hundred percent, but I'll bet it is."

"See, that's what I'm saying. You're almost always one move ahead of me."

"Only when it matters," I said, laughing. "Have you seen an image of it?"

"Yes. A small hologram."

"I haven't seen it, but, is it of a little girl, feeding ducks, not geese?"

"Oh! That's what was wrong! Something about it didn't seem quite right. The birds seemed too small. They were smaller than the little girl and, those geese —well, the little girl in this statue would be smaller than any one of Star's geese." He paused, his brow furrowing. "So, I give up. How do you know this?"

"I happened to be at Star's sanctuary when she got a call to go to Larry's pawnshop downtown, where he showed her a holo, no doubt, the holo you saw. It was small between them, so I couldn't see it. But soft-spoken Star read Larry the riot act for making her come down to look at a holo that wasn't even close to her Goose Girl Statue. She wanted to try to staunch any rumors or expansion of this false statue getting attention, but it looks like she did not succeed."

"Right. So, what does your intuition tell you about Larry?"

This surprised me, and I wasn't sure I wanted to discuss my first take on Larry, that he was in love with Star. And further, it seemed irrelevant. "Why do you ask?"

"He runs a pawnshop. Things are often found in pawnshops that belong to other people."

"Oh, right. Interesting." I had to think for a moment, as suddenly, I was hit with the question, what if Larry had taken the Goose Girl Statue? Why didn't that occur to me before?

"Why the hesitation?"

"I have to think it through. I guess you're saying it's a possibility that Larry took the Goose Girl Statue, and flaunts this other one to deflect any possible trail. He knows Star, he would know what the Goose Girl Statue is worth. It's interesting to contemplate."

"So... Regarding my question, what's your take on him?"

I shook my head. "I don't know. It isn't a thought that has crossed my mind, so I have to think it through. He seems like a nice guy."

"Wow, that's pretty weak." Travis made a face that I translated to mean something like, "it's not up to your usual standards." He reached out a foot and pushed on the glider, making it slide around cattywampas. I loved it!

Robbie poked his head out from under the blanket. "Hey! Cut it out!"

"The peanut gallery speaks!" Travis said, chortling.

"Oh, now, you two, don't get into it!" I ordered, not the least bit serious, but not wanting Robbie to be any more upset than he already was.

"Twice rude," Robbie sputtered. "Pushing Joy's glider around, and making a disparaging comment about me."

I reached down and petted him. "My dear little feline assistant, I rather much enjoyed the glider ride. But I take your side regarding Travis's rude comment to you." I looked at Travis with a small frown. "Do I have to drag out our old conversation, Travis, about not needlessly rubbing Robbie's fur the wrong way?"

"No, Joy, please don't. I'll behave."

"Good. Now, to return to our subject regarding Larry. I'm keeping some stuff to myself, while I sort it out." I *still* did not want to tell him it was obvious to me that Larry was in love with Star. Love can do all sorts of things, including revenge. Even though that sort of behavior does not fall under the heading of "love" in my book. The more I thought about Larry, with Travis sitting there staring at me, the more it seemed like he might be guilty of the theft of the Goose Girl Statue.

But I refused to say it out loud. As my mind thrashed around to come up with some other subject for the moment, perversely it came up with the forehead-to-forehead conversation he'd had with Elgin at Star's tea party. I do wish I'd let it go! If he didn't willingly share it with me, it was none of my business.

As if he read my mind, he said, "I had an interesting chat with that Ladybird the other evening at Star's. I don't know if you noticed we were engaged in a pretty intense conversation for a while."

I raised my eyebrows in an expression that I hoped looked something like, "Oh, really, I hadn't noticed." Now, is it a lie if you don't actually say an untruth out loud? But of course, as the gods and fate would decree, I was not about to find out about their conversation. A radio on him bleeped an arcane message, and he jumped up."Gotta go!"

"Right," I sighed in frustration, as I watched him leap down the two steps of the porch. Then he shocked me by turning around, jumping back up the two steps, dashing over to me, leaning down, and giving me a big hug. He turned again, and bounded down the two steps, calling over his shoulder, "Thanks for the break!"

He leapt into the Space XXX Roadster. A bolt of lightning and a crash of thunder accompanied the roar of his vehicle as it took to the skies.

Chapter 14
A Good Night's Sleep

Robbie came out from under the blanket. "That's better," he said very, very quietly.

"My dear furry friend, you will do well to bite the bullet and accept the continued reality of Travis in our lives."

Switching his tail, he stood on my out-stretched legs. "Yeah. Well. Anyway, changing the subject, what have you eaten today?"

"*Ahm* ..." I tried to think about what I'd had to eat. I had a vague memory of a very early breakfast with hot tea, some toast, and an orange. And then, not too long after that, having a cup of tea with

Goldie. *Holy tutti-frutti macaroni!* Was that today? It seemed like three days ago. Or a year.

A memorable day.

"I think I had some toast and tea and an orange, if that occurred today. It feels like ages ago. *What a day!* But you know what? I think I'll cook. Yes, that's what I'm going to do. I'm going to cook something."

"*Ahhhhhh*, you? Cook? Whoever you are, how dare you attempt to impersonate my Joy?"

Robbie had the ability to be a champion sardonic wit, and not even know it.

"Watch me." I made a move to stand, but Dickens gave me such a disapproving look, that I stopped in mid-motion. "All righty, I will cook in a little while, when Dickens is through with his nap."

"Oh! *Ha!* When Dickens is through with his nap? There is no such time. *This* is the Joy I know. The real question is *who* is going to cook? Why it's Robbie, the robot cat, without opposable thumbs. That's who."

I didn't know if I should laugh, or feel immensely sad. I kind of chuckled. "I *will* cook dinner. Something light and nutritious. But first, I'm still enjoying the lovely rain." I pulled the blanket up over my shoulders. "That was weird, that strike of lightning and clap of thunder when Travis left. The storm had passed, and yet, from nowhere, lightning and thunder."

"He probably made it happen to frighten me," Robbie murmured.

I laughed out loud. "You don't believe that, do you?"

"*You* believe in all sorts of paranormal phenomena. Why can't I?"

"Point taken. But, for the sake of argument, I suggest that Travis did not make it lightning and thunder when he left. Even if he could, he's nothing if not pragmatic. It would not be pragmatic to lift a flying car into a thunderstorm. Wouldn't you agree?"

"Are you trying to get away from the subject of saying you're going to cook dinner?"

"Probably. But let's cuddle here for a few minutes, while the rain taps out a percussion on the lilac and magnolia leaves."

"Ah, poetry," Robbie whispered, curling up and closing his eyes.

The next thing I knew, I was awakening from a deep, deep sleep, and night had fallen. Raindrops tap-tap-tapped all around the house, as if the fay were dancing on the leaves. I gathered up my two sleeping cats and the blanket, and went inside to bed. I put Robbie and Dickens side-by-side on the bed. Robbie had apparently decided to imitate Dickens to the limit of his ability. I looked longingly at the bed but realized I *really was hungry*. Even though intermittent fasting was healthy, I probably ought to eat something.

I dragged myself into the kitchen and resorted to my standby for the day—toast. I'd change it up by having peanut butter instead of apricot preserves. Or maybe, I thought, I'd go all out and have peanut butter *and* apricot preserves.

Hmmmm, now, where would the peanut butter be hiding? I opened up every cupboard and could not find it. I finally resigned myself to having it the next time. I knew where the bread and apricot preserves were, having had them in the long ago morning. I toasted two slices of bread, retrieved the apricot preserves, and sat at the kitchen table.

And what did I see? Lo-and-behold, I saw fruit! Right in front of me! After having Robbie bring it in from the dining room. I'd have some grapes! And even better than grapes, there were cherries in the bowl! How long had it been since I'd eaten cherries?

I did the equivalent of gorging myself on fruit and toast. Full beyond comfort, I shuffled into the bedroom and crashed into a deep, indulged-overeating sleep, with only a nightmare or two.

* *

I woke up after hours of deep, deep sleep. I stretched, looking down at the two cats, who were exactly where I'd placed them the night before.

Robbie jumped up. "Finally! A full, good night's sleep! Look at your bios, you haven't been this good in a long time. Maybe you'll take the day off and get a dynamic, first-class recharge."

"Not likely." I jumped out of bed. "Places to go. things to do." I tore around the bedroom, performing the essentials to make myself ready and presentable for the day. "No time to dawdle." I checked out the contents of my backpack, threw in my AR glasses, and scurried to the kitchen.

Oh no! I'd left a mess. Without Robbie picking up after me, since he'd stayed in bed with Dickens, my indulgent habits were left for me to witness.

Robbie came into the kitchen. "*Awk!* How does one person make such a mess in such a short while?"

"I wondered the same thing."

Robbie streaked around the kitchen, putting things in order. "I intended to ask you if you cooked dinner after all, but I don't see anything that implies you did some cooking."

I tried to recall what I'd been thinking, that I had turned the kitchen into such disarray. Then I re-membered—I couldn't find the peanut butter. "Rob-bie, where *is* the peanut butter? Yes, I was too tired to do anything that resembled cooking, so I got it in my head to have peanut butter on my toast, but I could *not* find it. I opened every cupboard, and apparently, I pulled out things without putting them back. No peanut butter."

Robbie jumped up on the counter and open the cupboard by the refrigerator. There sat the peanut butter.

"Oh! But I looked in that cupboard," I said, thoroughly bemused.

"Yes," Robbie agreed. "And here's all the stuff you pulled from the cupboard to prove it. Perhaps you want to accuse the peanut butter of being like the Goose Girl Statue, that it apported away while you looked for it, and now returned. Or the more likely reality, you looked right at it and didn't see it, because your mind was preoccupied. Because you were too tired. Because your body needed nutrition."

I was frowning. Frowning deeply. I had to accept that Robbie spoke the one-hundred percent truth. I'd been so distracted by everything, that I didn't see what was right in front of me, and in the process, I tore the kitchen apart. "You read me like a book, Robbie. Like an open book." I started to help him put things back in place.

"Oh please, Joy, just let me do it." Robbie took several things back out of where I stashed them and put them in other places. "I know you mean well, but let me maintain the order I've established in the kitchen. Well, quite frankly, in the whole house. If you start putting things in the wrong place, I won't be able to keep up."

Duly reprimanded, I toasted a slice of bread and, just to prove I could, I took the peanut butter out of the cupboard, slathered it on my toast, and returned it to its place. "It's more than a bit concerning that the peanut butter stood big-as-life right at my eye level, and I didn't see it. I cannot help but wonder how many other things I miss."

"I guess the advice might be," Robbie suggested, "that you remain particularly attentive today. It won't serve you to become hypervigilant, because that comes with its own set of complications. But ... be extra careful today."

I took his suggestion seriously. If my absent-minded professor habit dominated today, I might miss the "peanut butter" right in front of my eyes. "Noted, Robbie. Attentive without hypervigilance, good advice." I polished off my peanut butter toast, picked up my backpack, and headed for the back door, saying into my wrist comp, "Car, please come to the back door."

I climbed into the car without a single word, still contemplating my conversation with Robbie. My thoughts returned to the mystery of the missing Goose Girl Statue. Was there something right before my eyes that I missed, like the peanut butter?

I became so engrossed in my thought that I didn't notice the car had pulled out of the driveway and sat purring softly, at the roadside in front of my house.

"What's wrong?" I asked.

"You've not told me where to go, Dr. Forest."

Holy macaroni with cheese fries! What *was* the matter with me? Absent-minded, absent-minded, absent-minded! I allowed myself to be so busy thinking about being absent-minded, that I became yet more absent-minded. "Please take me to Star's sanctuary."

"Yes, Dr. Forest, we're on our way."

We soon arrived at Star's. There were a few cars in the parking lot, and I saw a small knot of people entering the little side door of the church. But the Drago caught my eye. None of the people entering the church was Zev. At the same time, I saw Star out in the pasture, riding her beautiful horse.

Where was Zev?

Chapter 15
Witnessing A Miracle

"**S**trange," I said reflectively, getting out of the car. I noted that there was a car by the Drago, and then four cars parked at a distance from those two. Two groups. The people I just saw walking in belonged to the four cars. Zev's Drago and the other car appeared to comprise another group.

Given that I could see Star riding her horse, Zev, and whoever accompanied him, were not with her. I headed for the little door, wondering why I had to have this negative thought about Zev. Perhaps, when I stepped inside, I'd see Zev with a friend treating some ailment in the healing light.

I hoped this would prove to be true.

But it did not. Inside, as my eyes adjusted to the subdued light, I saw the group of people standing around the Goose Girl Statue's residual healing light. I moved closer.

"Put your wrist in the light, William," a woman said.

"It seems ridiculous," the man I took to be William replied, holding onto his right wrist with his left hand, apparently in pain.

"It doesn't matter how it *seems*," another man said. "It only matters *what it is*."

William continued to hesitate.

"Next stop, surgery," the woman said, frustration and exasperation in her voice.

At this, William stuck his wrist into the light.

I was shocked by what I saw. His wrist looked to be swollen nearly three times its normal size, angrily purple, hanging at a wrong angle.

I gasped, and the other woman in their group glanced at me, but they were all focused on his wrist in the healing light. I moved a bit closer, and, before my very eyes, the wrist shrank down to its normal size, it moved into proper alignment, and the angry purple bruising faded.

"Wow!" William exclaimed in a quiet voice, "that's ... a miracle."

The first woman asked, "How do you feel?"

"I feel ... I feel no pain!"

Sensing that I invaded their private space, I crept around in the shadows toward the little room with the religious artifacts. Although still aglow with the miracle I'd just witnessed, I also had a not-good feeling about what I would now encounter.

I wasn't wrong.

I could hear voices in the religious artifact room, and, as I had predicted, one of them was Zev's. The door stood slightly ajar. I hoped I could make out what they said without being detected. Continuing in my sidling mode, I approached the door. Finally, I could make out their conversation.

"Altura, you're not to touch anything on this property. It's inappropriate for you to have come into this room. I don't appreciate having to chase after you. You said you wanted to experience the Goose Girl Statue's light, and that's why we're here. How do you even know about this room, I wonder?"

"*You* told me about it. You said there was some sort of light that could heal injuries, and that there was a room full of religious artifacts in this church."

"I told you about the light, but I don't recall telling you about this room. If I did, it was my mistake." He paused, and I could almost hear his cogs spinning. "Did you ... did you take the Goose Girl Statue?"

"What are you talking about?"

"The Goose Girl Statue is missing. Did you take her? We came here because you said you wanted to see if the Goose Girl Statue's light could help your elbow, which you say is injured. Maybe that's a line of BS."

"I don't know what you're talking about. You said there was a light here that healed injuries. I've been having pain in this damnable elbow. I didn't pay any attention to how you named the light, which is weird enough. This is the first time I've ever been here. Didn't you just see me stumbling down the crazy, dark halls and banging into the walls? Did it *look* like I've been here before?"

Zev sighed audibly. "Whatever. Let's get out of here."

The woman, apparently "Altura," laughed. "You must think I'm *so* stupid. But I'm not. I know who you are, Zev, and a leopard doesn't change his spots. I'm guessing you want all of this for yourself. There's probably a significant fortune in this room."

"For ... for...." Zev sounded so exasperated he couldn't even come up with an expletive. Too bad he didn't know me better, I could provide him with several creative exasperation relievers. "I am neither a leopard nor do I have spots."

"What*ever*," Altura retorted. "I know you want this all for yourself. You're becoming selfish. In the past, you would've happily shared this with me."

"The past is past. We are *done* with the past. Star is ... everything to me."

"Oh! First-class malarkey! She's no more your type than ... than ... a goose falls in love with a chicken. Plenty of both here, go out back and see for yourself. Would anybody believe that you fell in love with that scruffy little woman? And equally ridiculous, would anyone believe *she* had fallen in love with *you*? Yes, you're beautiful, but that's only skin deep. It's an easy bet that she's ten times more complicated than you, and, dear little manipulative boy, you won't convince me of your feigned innocence."

Even as she talked, I heard shuffling and clinking of the statuary being moved about, and I saw in my mind's eye this Altura person taking stock of what she saw in the room. My blood begin to boil, but I knew I had to remain unrevealed in order to get the most information out of this unpleasant, confrontational conversation.

I was torn. Was Altura right? Was Zev putting on an incredible show that Star—and even I—believed? Did he have in mind some massive heist of all these beautiful artifacts? Or did he truly love Star?

At this moment, that second option appeared pretty weak.

"I've had enough of your insults," Zev said in a low, approaching threatening, voice. "Get out now. I don't want to have to get physical."

Altura couldn't control her guffaw. "Oh, now you're too funny. Do you honestly think you could take me on? You weigh two-thirds of what I weigh, and as you know, I train daily."

"I suggest you don't push me to the point of discovering the damage I am capable of doing," he retorted in a subdued voice. "Anyway, threats are tacky, and I'm through making this one. Now, get out."

I heard shuffling, and I very much hoped that the next thing I heard would not be flesh encountering flesh.

"All right, all right," Altura said in a placating tone. "Don't get your undies in a bunch. I've gotten a good handle on what's here now, anyway."

"You don't need a handle on what's here. And what's here had better not disappear."

"I'll say the same to you, my dear little Zev. I'll be watching for any of these artifacts to appear on the market. You know me, you've worked with me, you know I have a photographic memory, even without my photographing implant."

I heard them move toward the door. I sank back into the shadows, coming to the little door on the other side of the church that I'd seen the pastor, all in black, leave the previous day. I slipped through the door, just as the door to the statuary room opened, hoping they did not see me.

Chapter 16
Dark Intentions

But this posed a new problem for me because now, I imagined, Zev would either be leaving or going out to the field to join Star. In either case, he'd see my car and would wonder where I was.

So, rather than coming around the front of the church and looking suspiciously as though I had come from where they had just been—which I did!—as Zev and Altura came out of the church from the other little door, or even worse, directly follow me through this little door, I turned to make my way around behind the church. An unpleasant stand of blackberries met my adventure. I managed to mostly skirt them, and with only a few minor impalements, I finally came out behind the barn.

I hoped Star wouldn't see me because she'd likely find it peculiar that I opted to take that challenging journey through the brambles. Fortunately, I saw her out on the land, on her beautiful black and white Indian spotted horse. Honestly, she was so beautiful, at one with her amazing creature. I leaned up against the barn as casually as the day is long. Then, I looked down at the several wounds I'd accumulated from my battle with the blackberries, one of the banes of my existence, and wiped away the blood on my forearms, hoping it would not reappear.

I chuckled, thinking that what I needed was to spend a few moments in the Goose Girl Statue's light.

Again, I hated to interrupt her, but under the circumstances, it became the only route open to me. She saw me, and waved. I waved back, watching as she spurred Banner toward the barn. He flew in a full run, a stunning sight to behold.

"Hi, Joy!" she called as they thundered up to the barn.

"Hi, Star. Fabulous to watch you on that gorgeous horse in a full-out run."

"Banner loves it when I let him completely open his throttle. What...."

At that moment, Zev came around the other side of the barn with Altura. Quite significant to see her, in the flesh. *Damn and hoodoo! An Amazon!* I wouldn't want to meet her in a dark alley. No wonder she laughed at Zev when he threatened to take her on.

Following my glance, Star turned to look behind her. "Hey, Zev!" she said, a bit of surprise in her voice.

"Hey, Star," Zev answered, "Hey."

There again, I noted his conspicuous shyness in the presence of Star. But! *Was* it shyness? Or guilt because he knew he was going to do her wrong? I hated the lack of clarity I had around these questions.

"I didn't want to bother you," Zev said. "I brought Altura to experience the healing light because she said she injured her elbow in some sort of Athletic mishap."

"Oh," Star said simply. I watched as she took in Altura, a good foot-and-a-half taller than Zev. "Is your elbow better?" Star asked.

Caught off guard by the question, Altura frowned slightly then smiled hugely. Oh, really scary sight, inauthentic and full of a brace of too-big, and it even seemed like too many, teeth. No, no, wouldn't wanna meet her in a dark alley.

The thought that she and Zev were historically, even if not currently, in cahoots, was dark and unpleasant.

"Oh, yeah, my elbow. Better. Much better." She waved her left arm around. "Not perfect, but better."

Goodness! She was a very bad liar. Even I could tell she was fabricating. I wondered how this interaction struck Star. Something crossed her features. I surmised it to be her ca-ca detector. "That's good," she said without inflection.

No. She did not believe Altura. And what effect did it have on her feelings for Zev?

I looked at Zev. *Aha!* He saw Star did not believe her.

He did a quick save. "Why are you saying that, Altura? We haven't gotten to the light yet, as there've been other people in front of us."

Altura laughed nonchalantly. "True, that. I … didn't want to disappoint you, Star."

Well now, *none* of us believed *that*.

"I see the other people are leaving," Star said as she looked toward the parking lot.

Standing behind the barn, I couldn't see the activity, but I heard car doors closing, along with exclamations of surprise and happiness. I couldn't contain my amazement. "I just saw a miracle, Star. A man in the group had a badly injured wrist, horribly swollen, dark, angry purple, and out of alignment.

"For some strange reason, he didn't want to put his wrist in the light. But a woman in the group pragmatically said, 'next stop, surgery.' That lit a fire under him, and he put his wrist in the light, and in moments it returned to its normal dimension, its normal alignment, and the purple faded. So amazing! But I felt I was invading their private space, so I came out here to watch you riding, Star. As I said, such a beautiful sight."

I couldn't resist pushing at the dark intentions of Zev and his "friend." "But, Zev, I didn't see you in there." This was true, I hadn't seen them. Heard plenty, though.

Altrua took over. "Oh, you missed us there in the pews in the shadows. We saw you come in. We saw you watch that man's miracle, and then come back outside."

Boy oh boy! Ghee would not melt in her mouth, that's how cold she was.

An awkward silence fell among us. Then Altrua said, "Nice chatting, but I really gotta get back to work. I'm a trainer at *Your Best Body*, and my clients are wondering where I am. I'll have to come back some other time to see if this miracle light can help my elbow. Bye now."

Without waiting for a reply, she turned and strode away. I hoped far, far away. If I never saw her again, it would suit me fine.

The awkwardness continued between Star and Zev.

I, for one, wanted badly to get into that religious relic room, and take a detailed inventory, recording and picturing, and sending it to my computer at home, with Robbie making sure it appeared complete and intact. At this moment, I didn't trust either of those two people farther than I could throw them. Well, Zev I could heave some good distance. But Altrua, I probably couldn't get her feet off the ground. In any case, I wouldn't want to touch her.

I found it significant that Star did not get off her horse. Then some eye-talk went on between Star and Zev. Zev cocked his head, and said, "I've got work to do, too. See you soon, Star."

"All right, Zev. I'll see you soon."

He turned and walked toward his car. I moved to the edge of the barn to watch him. I wanted to see his body language. His shoulders were slumped, and he walked slowly. He was truly depressed. However, that did not clarify for me if he felt guilty. Depressed because he had damaged his relationship with Star?

Or depressed because his cover had been blown?

Chapter 17
Experiencing A Miracle

Star and I exchanged a look, while I contemplated telling her about what I'd overheard in the religious artifacts room. I decided to hold on to that information for a little while. I wanted to take an inventory of the statuary in that room, and Star, who had still not gotten down from Banner, wanted to continue her ride, it seemed obvious. She also probably needed to think through what she'd encountered with Altura and Zev.

I was open to talking about it, but Star was not.

"I think I'll go back inside and spend some time with the light, as I had originally intended, now that there appears to be no one there," I said.

"Good idea," Star agreed, reigning Banner around and riding out onto the property at a slow canter.

I watched her for a few moments, thinking everything through, then returned to the church, entering through the little door that was *not* impeded by blackberry bushes. I passed the soft glow of the light bathing the Goose Girl Statue's stand, and headed directly for the religious artifacts room in the near darkness of the unlighted halls.

Entering the room, I saw a path through the middle of the statuary, where the nearly giant Altura had been making her way through the statues. It made for me a project as I would have to do a lot of shuffling of these heavy statues in order to produce an inventory, since they were now slammed up against one another.

"Robbie, I need you to ensure that the inventory I'm about to make is perfectly entered into the computer and your database." His hologram furry face popped up in front of me.

"Oh boy! I'm on it!" Robbie loved nothing better than to help me when I was away from home.

I started in the far back corner, and, although the statues were heavy, and although I had very little space to work in, I made good progress, taking 3-D vids and having Robbie make details of measurements and materials, and any other distinctive feature of each piece. Before long, I came to the path Altura had made. I noted that a particularly beautiful alabaster statue of St. Francis stood in the middle of this path. I took extra photos and 3-D video and Robbie carefully noted measurements and other details.

I moved to the back of the room, to continue the inventory. I grabbed onto a particularly large statue of Green Tara. An amazingly beautiful work of art, a delicate shade of green, but so incredibly heavy. As I leaned her away from the neighboring statue, she came back on my fingers, crushing them between the two statues.

"*Ohhhh*," I said softly as pain coursed through my entire body like I had never felt in my life.

"*What?*" Robbie cried. "What happened? I can't see. What happened?"

I tried not to make a huge exclamation that would disturb him, but, of course, his hook-up to my bios let him know something terrible had occurred.

"I... I... appear to have crushed a couple fingers between these two statues." I dared to look down at my two fingers, and nearly fainted. They were bent almost ninety degrees the wrong way. A wave of nausea passed through me. I breathed heavily, hoping to calm the waves of pain.

"Yes, yes, Joy, you've severely hurt yourself. Perhaps more than you realize. You need immediate medical attention. I'm calling 911."

"No, Robbie. No." The pain pulsed, becoming yet more excruciating. I had a hard time thinking. "Wait just a minute." Why did I tell him to wait?

"I don't want to wait, Joy. You might pass out."

Then it came to me, the thought trying to make its way through the pain, that the Goose Girl Statue's light shone in the sanctuary, and, if I could make it there without passing out, I could run my own experiment about the healing light. "I'm heading back to the Goose Girl Statue's healing light. Let's see if it works. If I faint between here and there, call for help."

I turned to make my way back through the halls and, cleverly enough, Robbie made a light of his hologram so I could see my way. I finally came to the Good Girl Statue's stand, and, most peculiarly, I had the same reaction that William—a stranger to me—had. I resisted putting my profoundly damaged, and unendurably painful fingers into the light.

"What's wrong?" Robbie demanded. "Why aren't you putting your fingers in the light?"

"I ... I don't know. I'm sensing the strongest resistance to doing it. It's quite strange."

"If you don't put your fingers in the light right now, I'm contacting help," Robbie said in an authoritative voice that I had never heard from him. My response was to stick my hand in the light.

An utterly strange sensation coursed through me. I could feel my fingers straightening, but throughout my entire body I felt a flow of energy, and ... most unexpected, I felt ... love. Warm, unconditional, and like nothing I'd ever felt. Love ... the force behind the creative force. In that moment, I knew more than I had ever learned in my whole life.

"*Zowie!*" Robbie whispered. "Your bios are doing something I've never seen any human bios do."

"True. And like I've never felt."

Robbie and I watched my fingers as they moved of their own accord into proper alignment. The unbearable pain totally disappeared.

"Amazing," Robbie said. "Unbelievably amazing."

"Yes," I agreed. And, as I watched, my wounds from the blackberry brambles also disappeared before my eyes. "Wow, and wow again!"

"*Now* what happened?" Robbie asked. "Something else is going on with your bios."

"Right. I got some scratches and puncture wounds from the blackberries going out to the barn. They just closed up and disappeared as if they never happened." I moved to the front pew and sat down, completely overwhelmed.

"Why were you walking through blackberries?" Robbie asked. "Never mind telling me right now. Come home and tell me more."

I gathered myself and stood. "I have to finish the inventory first."

"What!! Oh no, you're not. You're coming home now and recouping."

"I don't need to recuperate, I'm fine. I need to get the inventory done."

"If you don't come home right now, I am coming there." Robbie manifested his whole body in his hologram, swishing his tail.

"You're not going to do that." I shook my head, disbelieving his behavior.

"*Oh yes, I am!*" He headed for the back door, opened it, and stepped out on the step. "I *am* coming," he repeated.

Holy rustling cattails! He was serious! I couldn't have my robot out wandering the streets. "Goodness!

Relax, Robbie. I'll come home if you're going to be so darn insistent. Give me a light back to the holy relics room so I can close the door, and I'll come home."

He projected a light back through the hallways, and I did as I said I would, closing the door when I got there, though peeking in and making a mental note of how many statues had yet to be inventoried. Probably about a dozen. I knew I dared not do anything but close the door, or he'd be out on the road.

I had never seen this behavior from him, ever.

Then I turned and went back down the hall, with Robbie shining the light for me. I paused before the Goose Girl Statue's stand, contemplating the light. "Thank you," I said simply. "Thank you so much ... for the healings and for the sensation of pure unconditional love." I meditated for a moment, even as I sensed Robbie tapping his little clawed foot, watching to make sure I would do as I said.

I went outside and got in the car. "Home, please."

"I'm somewhat aware of what just transpired," the car said, pulling out onto the road. "As I'm hooked up to your wrist comp and the home computer. It seems you've had an injury, and you've had a healing."

"Yes. I broke a couple fingers moving statues around. The Goose Girl Statue's light healed my fingers, right before my eyes, and some blackberry scratches I'd acquired, too."

"Miraculous," the car said.

I nodded. "Truly miraculous."

Chapter 18
Lovely Lentil Soup

When I got home, Robbie fussed around me like a little old grandmother. I can't say I minded, because, although completely healed of both the broken fingers and, *bonus!*, the blackberry bramble stabs, I felt strangely exhausted. I'd begun to suspect the healing process actually did require the body to continue to do its work that it does best when one sleeps.

Robbie made a little bowl of lentil soup and a lovely avocado sandwich. I sat at the kitchen table watching him making magic of putting things together while commanding all the devices in the kitchen like a captain at the helm of a ship. I hardly knew how the devices worked, but Robbie appeared as if he had invented them.

I put my head down on my crossed forearms and surprised myself by falling directly asleep. Robbie had to prod me awake.

"See? I was right. You needed to come home after that experience."

Something smelled wonderful, and I raised my head to see the rich lentil soup steaming in front of me. I sat up and wolfed it down as if I'd not eaten in a year, then launched into doing similar damage to the avocado sandwich. "I'm not gonna argue with you, Robbie. You were right. I was just thinking about how my body is continuing the healing process, which, of course, it does best during sleep. And nutrition doesn't hurt either." To prove my point, I polished off the sandwich, followed by a lovely glass of water.

"My goodness, Joy, would you like some more?"

"No, Robbie, I'm good for the moment. But that was really, really perfect, thank you."

I petted him between his ears, and his purring vibrated right through my hand. He did love to please me and to get positive reinforcement.

"All right, my friend, I'm off to bed. Though it's only early evening, I feel sleep is on the agenda. My schedule is all over the place these days." Robbie and I went into the bedroom, where Dickens, predictably, already kept his spot warm, sound asleep in the middle of the bed. Soon the lights were out, and so was I.

But I awoke with a start a few hours later. I found myself compelled to complete the inventory of the religious relics. I looked at the time. Two a.m. I did a bit of math. I'd been sleeping for six hours. Good enough! I jumped up from the bed, threw on the clothes I'd abandoned a few hours before on the back of the chair, pulled on a jacket, threw my backpack over my shoulder, and headed for the back door.

Robbie leapt up from the bed. "Where are you going? What are you doing? It's the middle of the night."

"Don't try to stop me, Robbie. I've had six really solid good hours of sleep, and I need to get back to the inventory of the religious relics. I'm wide awake obsessing about it, and you know me, Robbie. Once I get something in my mind, I have to deal with it. I'm not going to get back to sleep."

"Why so urgent? Certainly, it could wait until morning. Plus, won't you disturb Star, thrashing around on her property in the middle of the night?"

I hadn't thought of that. The truth is, I didn't know where she slept. I hadn't seen a bedroom in the rooms I'd passed. But Robbie made a good point, and I was glad he mentioned it.

"I'll go in the little back door, and be very quiet. I'll whisper the information to you, and we'll finish up the project. I don't trust that Altura person, and Star doesn't have *any* security that I saw. I need to get those artifacts photographed and their details recorded. I don't think that will disturb Star. When I'm done with the inventory of the few remaining religious statues, I'll come right back home."

"Car, please come to the back door," I said into my wrist comp as I stepped out, Robbie on my heels. "Standby, Robbie, let's get this project done." I jumped into the car. "Star's sanctuary," I said.

"On our way." The car pulled out onto the road and hummed along. "You do know it's two-fifteen, in the middle of the night, Dr. Forest."

"I do."

"All right, then. As long as you realize you're going to someone's home at a generally perceived inappropriate time."

"I have to get the inventory of the religious relics done. Not going to sleep until it is."

"Yes, Dr. Forest. And disturbing Miss Moon?"

"I don't think I will. Although I don't know where she sleeps, I think I can slip into the little back side door, take the images and whisper the details to Robbie, and have the job complete in a few minutes. Miss Moon is very trusting. But I am not!"

We came into the church's parking lot. "Pull around to the other side of the church, so I'm closer to the little door on the other side."

The car drove around to the far side of the church. I couldn't believe what I saw!

And yet ... I could....

Chapter 19
Stealing St. Francis

There stood a huge, black, enclosed truck, its motor running.

"Go back around to the other side of the church, and get as close to the little door as you can," I said to the car.

I put on my AR glasses as the car did as I bid, I soon jumped out and entered the darkened church through the little door, then tiptoed through the darkness past the Goose Girl Statue's stand with its soft light, and crept down the hall. Fortunately, my AR glasses made the surroundings light enough that I could see where I was going.

I dreaded to see Zev in the religious relics room, but I knew for sure I would encounter Altura. Slinking up to the half-open door, I saw her standing beside the St. Francis statue. I looked around the room as much as I could see with the partially open door, and did not see Zev, or anyone else.

Robbie, able to see everything I could see, whispered in my ear, "I'm calling Travis! Don't argue!"

I wasn't about to argue. I wondered why I hadn't already done it myself, except I'd gotten caught up in the moment. I nodded. Robbie would be able to see and understand that motion via my AR glasses.

I tried to calculate how long I had before Travis arrived, but that was an exercise in futility because one never knew how far away he might be, or how engaged in stopping a crime.

"Come with me, my lovely," Altura said to the beautiful St. Francis statue. "I will free you from this prison. Someone may well put you in their garden, wouldn't you like that? And I ... who knows what advantages freeing you might be for me? I have no idea what you're worth, but I'll soon find out." She hefted up the statue, and started to take him out of the room.

I shrank back into the shadows, trying to convince myself to wait for Travis. But when Altura was almost at the little door, and soon St. Francis would be in that big black truck, I could not hold on another moment. Plus, I knew I had the advantage of surprise.

I leapt out of the shadows and flew to the little back door. With Altura's back to me, I had the advantage. But I didn't want to risk damaging the St. Francis statue. Although Altura was gigantic, I, myself, at five-foot-eleven, I hoped, was a near match for her.

I wrapped my arm around her neck. "Let go of St. Francis," I hissed in her ear.

"What the...." she squawked as I closed the air off her windpipe.

"What the 'what' is, you're not stealing any of these religious artifacts. Let go of St. Francis." I tightened my grip on her throat.

She put St. Francis down, and I thought triumphantly, *yay! That was easy!* A wildly premature thought. Her prodigious strength overcame me, and she soon faced me, turning the tide on who had the upper hand. "Oh! It's you! What the hell are you doing here in the middle of the night?"

As she had her hand around my throat, I couldn't answer her. But I *did* feel it was rather obvious. Oh, why hadn't I waited for Travis? Surely he would be here any moment now.

As consciousness begin to ebb from the inability to breathe, I made a desperate effort to knock her off her footing, shoving into her with all my might. At the same time, I couldn't take my mind off the St. Francis statue immediately behind her, which our scuffling threatened to knock over.

I stepped back, but Altura stuck to me like glue. I at least gained a small bit of breathing room, and with that, I gathered my forces. With both arms free, I reached up and pushed on her shoulders—like trying to move a cement wall! That girl was solid!

"I don't understand how you can be here in the middle of the night!" she yelled in my ear, releasing her hold on my throat in order to grab onto my arms. "I checked the place out. There's no surveillance anywhere that I can see. Plus, I just got here." She now had my arms pinned. The only option left open to me was to attempt to push her with all my strength, the both of us going down together, and hopefully, wrest myself free.

"Or maybe," she said, as if with some great insight, "you're here to do what I'm doing! That's it!"

I realized there was no future in engaging in conversation with her, but this pushed all my buttons. "No, crazy woman, everyone in the world is not a criminal like you! Now, take your hands off me. The police are on their way and you are not going to win this round." I gathered my forces to bulldoze my entire weight into her. But still, she didn't budge.

"Nice try ..." she cackled. "I've got your number! You had in mind to make your own heist. But that's not going to happen. Before this night is over, you're going to find yourself floating face down in the Columbia River. Too bad. So sad."

I thrust my body weight into her again, but she was like a massive statue herself! I only managed to accomplish a weird little two-step, backing up and once again, coming into the range of potentially knocking over St. Francis, who stood there, facing us, equal to our heights, patiently watching the whole fiasco.

As I looked at him, much to my shock, he began to rock although we'd not touched him. Suddenly, he came forward, slamming into Altura.

Chapter 20
St. Francis to the Rescue

She yelled, releasing her hold of me. Down she went, St. Francis across her body. She struggled to get up but, she wasn't going anywhere!

At the same moment, I heard a rumbling overhead, and the echoing of Clark County's finest, detective Travis Rusch, announcing in a voice that could be heard for blocks, "Clark County police!"

I heard the Space XXX Roadster come to the ground, and, in my mind's eye, I saw it landing in front of the big black truck that would not be going anywhere with any religious relics this night.

Sirens and the slam of car doors surrounded the church. Soon, police came in both little doors of the church, led by Detective Travis Rusch. He dashed through the little door, ran up to me, and grabbed me.

"Are you all right?" he asked, concern in his voice and anxiety on his features.

"Yes, Travis, yes, I'm all right." I gestured to the floor, "St. Francis came to the rescue!"

We looked down at Altura, who continued to struggle under the weight of St. Francis, calmly lying across her from hip to shoulder, arms and body pinned. She was swearing a blue streak, which we both chose to ignore.

"This is Altura—I met her earlier today. I just now caught her red-handed, trying to walk out with St. Francis. He has reciprocated by pinning her to the floor."

Travis tried unsuccessfully to stifle a guffaw. "That's a remarkable use of a religious statue, I must say." He turned to a couple of the officers rushing up to us. "Officer White and Officer Tolleson, please relieve St. Francis of his duties here." He gestured to Altura under St. Francis.

"Yes, sir." The two officers came forward, one stood St. Francis up, and the other stood Altura up.

Another officer hurried up behind me. "Would you like me to attend to this suspect as well, Officer Rusch?" he asked, gesturing to me.

"Oh! No, Officer Johnston, that's Joy ... I mean, that's Dr. Forest," Officer Tolleson exclaimed.

Travis let go of me.

Officer Johnston's comment caused me to burst into silly giggles, though I was disappointed to have Travis let me go.

"Oh! So sorry Dr. Forest. S ... s...sorry!" he stuttered, confused and embarrassed.

"Unless there's something, Officer Johnston, you know about Dr. Forest that I don't," Travis commented, a wry grin growing on his features.

This elicited a guffaw from the officers filling the transept area of the church.

"Okay, enough levity," Travis said. "Officer Tolleson, take the suspect outside and read her her rights," he said over her whining and complaining at the top of her voice, insisting that she'd done nothing wrong.

Unfortunately, I realized she was pretty much correct. She'd been found attempting to steal St. Francis, but she didn't get out the door with him. So there wouldn't be much to go on.

"Right, Officer Rusch," Officer Tolleson said as he issued her out the door.

Travis turned to me. "Here's your Goose Girl Statue thief."

"I ... I don't think so, Travis."

"*What!* Why not?"

"Because I listened to her talking to Zev earlier today, and she didn't know anything about the missing Goose Girl Statue. It was pretty obvious, from the way the subject came up from Zev, when he accused her."

"How much water does a conversation like that hold?"

"I know it'd make things easier if it was her. But I just ... don't feel it." I still missed something.

"You don't feel it. I'm going to run a lie detector test on her." He stepped to the little door. "Officer Tolleson, please take the suspect to the Roadster. I want to give her a lie detector test."

Travis stepped out. That was when a terrible thought hit me.

Where was Star?

How could she possibly sleep through all this hubbub and melodrama? My blood ran cold recalling how easily Altura threatened my life—what if she'd done harm to Star?

"*I must find Star! I must find Star!*" I turned to start tearing through the church ... and ran right into Star.

"Why must you find me? And why must you re-peatedly run headlong into me?"

"Here you are! Thank goodness! Sorry about the weird running into you, again and again! I had to find you because ... I ... I figured anyone who could sleep through all this hullabaloo and pandemonium might not be... sleeping. How *did* you sleep through the racket?"

"I don't usually sleep in the church. I have a very nice little room," she waved in a vague direction. "But I have a cot in the barn, and I like to sleep out there, with my creatures. I heard the hullabaloo as you call it, but I'm a deep sleeper, and when the noise finally got my attention, I assumed—because I didn't want to wake up—that it was at a neighbor's house."

"Even though you don't have any neighbors for blocks."

"Even though. As I said, I sleep deeply."

Travis came back through the little door. "Hello, Star. I was wondering where you were. You must sleep very soundly to sleep through all this noise!"

I nodded my silent agreement.

"I do, and also, I sleep in the barn," Star answered.

"You need to have security. I don't see any security anywhere. You're very fortunate Joy happened to be here and apprehended a highly experienced thief, caught in the act."

"Altura," Star said simply.

"Yes. Altura. Do you know her?"

"No. But I met her this afternoon."

"Just this afternoon?"

"Yes."

She said nothing more.

"Star, you have to tell him the truth," I insisted.

"What truth?" Travis asked.

Star hesitated, but finally said, "She was here with Zev. She told him she had an injury to her elbow, and she wanted to see if the Goose Girl Statue's light would do anything for it."

"What is Zev doing with a character like that?" Travis asked in an undertone.

"I believe they used to be partners," Star answered. "But ... and you can believe me or not, I have no control over that ... they are no longer associated. I saw that Altura was working a number on Zev, but he wasn't falling for it."

Travis shook his head. "It'll come out in the end, you know, Miss Moon, don't you?"

"I do indeed," she said with a quiet affirmation that let me know she was well apprised of everything swirling around her. Better than Travis. Better than I.

"But you must have security, Miss Moon. I hope this night's events make that clear to you," Travis all but wagged his finger.

Star gestured to me. "Joy was my security, as you see. Considerably better than any mechanical security one could come by."

Travis raised his eyebrows. "But Joy is not your security." He turned to me. "Unless there's a relationship I don't know about. Joy, have you taken on the responsibility of security here?"

I shook my head. "Negative, Travis." That's a job I'd *never* take *anywhere*, even here at the lovely creature sanctuary. I loved it, but, no, I wouldn't spend eight hours a night, night after night, watching for the likes of future Alturas.

"I'm confused by your statement, Miss Moon," Travis said, a perplexed frown working across his forehead.

"You're missing the power of the statues. If you'd think about it, you'd realize that the value in that statuary room is tremendous, and it would have been ripped off years ago, even before I owned this property, if not for the fact that the supernatural energy of the religious statuary bears a self-protecting energy that will call to it what it needs."

Now she made me think! Although I'm known to obsess on a project like I had earlier in the night to come and finish the inventory—that could absolutely have waited until morning—the grinding, pushing urge that woke me and compelled me until I arrived here in time to save St. Francis ... was maybe not all just my own energy.

Star turned to me. "I told you I saw you in a vision before you came. When you came, you saw a flash of light. That let me know you were the one I'd seen in my vision. I knew you had come to provide some protection for the sanctuary. And here you are. And so you did."

I thrust my hands up in a dramatic gesture, shrugging. "And here I am, and so I did. I don't think anyone can argue that fact."

Travis shook his head. "I'm out of my woo-woo league, as usual, when Joy's involved."

"This is pretty advanced for my league, too, Travis. But I think Star knows the statuary better than we do, and I'd say, don't mess with a system that's working."

"I can only advise according to my own training, knowledge, and experience," Travis said. "Which does not include a paranormal component. Thus, I must enter into the report that I have advised you to install security."

Star frowned.

"I know. You believe the statuary *itself*, is an installation of security. I do appreciate your beliefs. And my attempting to point out that the Goose Girl Statue remains at large, also carries no weight with you. That is, if you still believe it has apported?"

"I believe the Goose Girl Statue has moved without being stolen."

"Yes. As you say. Well, our business is done here, and we'll be on our way." He nodded to me. "We'll talk soon."

"Looking forward to it. Not about apporting though, right?"

"Decidedly." He made for the little door, where St. Francis stood sentry. "I assume this statue was not in this location. Would you like it returned to wherever it had been? Or will it apport on its own?"

"That would be fantastic, Detective Rusch," I said. "Though the sarcasm is probably not necessary."

"*Hmmm* ... you're right, Joy. I apologize, Miss Moon. Officer Tolleson, help me return this statue...."

"It's St. Francis," I said. I could not stand to hear "this statue" one more time about the beautiful, and, secretly animate, alabaster St. Francis.

"Help me return St. Francis to wherever he came from."

"Yes, sir."

The two of them hefted St. Francis, and I led them through the halls to the religious relics room.

"If you don't mind, I believe I'll go back to bed," Star called after us.

"Yes, please do," Travis said. "Sweet dreams," he added.

Chapter 21
Gentle Light on the Horizon

"Oh, Travis!" I said, surprised and pleased. "That was ... *sooo lovely!* You don't always have to be a curmudgeon."

"I'm *not* a curmudgeon. I'm professional."

"Yes. That too. You heard nothing, Officer Tolleson."

"Deaf as a statue," Officer Tolleson agreed. "Or maybe *more* deaf than a statue."

They were both breathing heavily by the time we got to the religious relics room. I thought about how Altura carried it practically with ease, and re-minded myself I was lucky to be breathing.

I opened the door to the little statue-filled room and turned on the light.

"Holy saints among us," Officer Tolleson cried at the sight. "What an incredible collection. It feels...."

"Are you ... a sensitive?" I asked.

"Well, I'd think just about anyone would be, with this much energy floating around."

"What about you, Travis?"

"Let's set St. Francis down," he said rather much ignoring my question.

"Just put him here in this open space," I pointed. They set St. Francis down. I reached out and patted his alabaster shoulder. "Thank you for what you did earlier."

Travis looked at me quizzically, but I opted to spare him any more "woo-woo" this night. "The contents of this room are more than one can take in, in one fell swoop," Travis said. "To answer your question, Joy, no, I cannot say I'm 'a sensitive.' That's better left to you. I don't think it's an attribute I can develop. But you have it, and I don't argue that fact.

"All right, I gotta get on the road. Or in the air, more accurately. Places to go, things to do, crime to stop."

I walked with the two of them back to the little door. "Good night Dr. Forest," Officer Tolleson said, giving me a salute with a great, big grin. "This is going to go down in my memoir as one of my favorite jobs! And no bloodshed. Thanks for the experience."

"Sure. My pleasure. You know, Officer Tolleson, you can come back any time you want and sit in the religious relics room. Miss Moon has an open door policy about the church, the Goose Girl Statue's healing light, and the religious relics room."

"Oh! That's awesome! I'd like to do that sometime. What a great way to meditate. Thanks again." He ambled off into the night.

"The same goes for you, Travis, you're welcome to sit in that room and see what energy might come up."

"I'm not against the notion. I might do that sometime. It seems to me, that to take the time to look at each of the statues, to think about all of the various times in history they represent, their ethnic backgrounds, and the heartfelt intention of the people who carved and created them ... even if I didn't have a paranormal experience, I'm sure it would be meaningful." He gave me a quick hug and turned, making his way to his vehicle.

That sight never hurt my eyes in the least. Travis looked great, coming or going. "Thank you, Travis," I called after him, "for once again saving my life!"

He waved his hand over his head, without turning around. "Any time, Joy. Any time."

I noted that the Space XXX Roadster was in a slightly different location, accounting for the thieving big black truck having been seized and removed.

Well! Now then! I could get back to what I came here to do. Finish my inventory.

"You there, Robbie?"

"Every beat of the way. *What* an adventure."

"Yes, yes, and *yes*. All's well that ends well."

"The most important part. I was at my wits' end when that giant woman had her hand around your throat."

"Pretty much at my wits' end too! And nearly my breathing end, as well!"

"Thank goodness for St. Francis."

"Oh yes, thank goodness for St. Francis! And for Travis."

"I guess so," Robbie said begrudgingly. "A little bit."

"You gotta like him!" I teased.

"No, I don't. Let's get to work."

I spent another hour or so finishing the inventory of the statues. Then I sat in the little chair and spent some quiet time with them. The energy was invigorating and relaxing at the same time. But most of all, I experienced an overwhelming sense of *love*.

It just doesn't get any better than that.

I finally stood, turned out the light, closed the door, and walked through the halls to the delicate bit of light cast from the stained glass windows in the pre-dawn light.

I stepped through the little door to the outside. "Come around to the other little door," I called to the car, entirely too lazy to walk around the church in the semi-darkness to where I'd left the car.

As I stood breathing deeply, monumentally enjoying the early, early morning breeze, and the gentle peach light filtering along the horizon, I saw a figure in black at the bottom of the hill. I watched as he took in my car, moving around the church. He stopped, then turned around.

My presence disrupted his meditation. Another thought crossed my mind. "Peanut butter," I whispered.

Chapter 22
Celestial Music

The car pulled up, and I got in.

"Home? It's been a long night."

"It *has* been a long night, that's true. But it's not over yet. Take a right out from the church and then the next right. And drive slowly."

"Yes, Dr. Forest." The car did as I bid. We ambled along as if we had no agenda. The road was almost completely ours, but I wished there was a bit of traffic for cover. Before long I saw the man in black, limping slightly, with umbrella in hand for a cane. We came alongside him.

We passed him slowly, and I didn't look at him, but I had my wrist comp trained on him, and I watched as he watched me drive by.

"Anything, in particular, you're looking for about this man in black?"

"I'd like to know where he lives."

"You will see that shortly," the car said.

We came to a huge complex of small apartments and soon drove by the decorative scenery the complex had in front. There were deer and raccoons and rabbits, a big fake tree with a big fake owl and it. Water poured over a rocky waterfall, with flowers and ferns all around.

All well and good and pretty. But marring the entire scene, a gigantic sign across the center, declared, "Home at Last!" Under that, "The Best Retirement Home Anywhere! Gold in Your Golden Years!"

"What*ever*," I said. I rarely drove by here, but that sign always got under my skin. For one thing, it lacked class. For another thing, what did 'gold in your golden years' even mean?!?

I found it patronizing. If they just had the scenery without all that babble, I would have thought more of it. But then again, they didn't ask me.

We'd driven by the complex, over two blocks long.

"There he goes," the car said.

Goodness! I'd gotten so caught up in my critiquing the sign that I already knew I didn't like, I forgot the project at hand.

"Turn around, and let's see if we can find him." The car u-turned and went back to where the man in black had gone into the complex. "Pull over and kill the engine."

The car did as I asked.

"Roll down my window." Sitting inside the car, with the window down, I listened. Soon I heard what I was listening for—a slow tapping of the umbrella. I got out of the car. "Don't go anywhere."

"No plans to," the car replied.

I followed the tap-tapping sound. But then it stopped. I didn't know which way to turn in the veritable labyrinth of parking stalls. I could only follow my intuition, which seemed at the moment to be asleep. In addition, I felt more than strange creeping around in a retirement home roadway in the wee hours of the morning.

But wait! I heard someone talking softly. I moved toward the sound, and before long I came to a parking stall where stood the man in black in front of the closed doors of a storage space. "I think I've done wrong to have you here," he said. "There's no point in it, it doesn't make a difference. But it was so tricky to get you here, and I don't think I have the energy to take you back on my own."

He recited a series of numbers. The locking device clicked, and the doors to the storage unit opened slightly. Through the crack, a glorious light shone. I could barely see a sliver of the indescribably beautiful Goose Girl Statue, glowing in that light I had already become familiar with in Star's church.

I felt ecstatic to hear what he said because I had the solution to his dilemma. But I must not scare him to death, sneaking up on him. Strangely enough, I'd not heard his name, certain that Star had never mentioned it.

"Hello," I called softly.

The man jumped, slamming the storage space doors shut. I heard the locks engage.

"Who are you?" he demanded, and justifiably so. How often does a person in their own private retirement home parking stall at 4:30 a.m. expect to be accosted?

"My name is Joy Forest, Dr. Joy Forest. I'm not too sure exactly how to approach this ... although I usually find it effective to commence with the truth...."

"Well then, kindly voice that, and stop babbling. Are you lost?"

"No. No, I ... I want to help you. I have a solution to your dilemma."

"What dilemma?" The man in black started to become a bit angry.

Not the most long-suffering way to present for a pastor, I thought fleetingly. However, one had to have some compassion for him having been snuck up upon.

"Yes. To get to the point. I will help you get the Goose Girl Statue back on her stand."

He breathed a visible sigh of relief. "I don't know how you figured out that I have it, but thank you. I gratefully accept your offer to assist me."

"Car, come to me."

The car honed in on my coordinates and appeared directly.

"Do you think the two of us can handle this by ourselves, and will she fit in the back of my car?"

"Yes, and yes. She is surprisingly light, and the back of your vehicle is the perfect size for her."

I had the car back into the storage space.

"By the way, what is *your* name?"

"Reverend William Westell. Please call me Bill."

"So very pleased to meet you, Reverend Westell ... Bill. Now, let's see if we can succeed in getting the gorgeous and beloved Goose Girl Statue into my car."

He unlocked and fully opened the storage space doors. I gasped and fell back against my car. The statue was too beautiful. Absolutely impeccable beauty. I felt tears start, which shocked me, because I never cry.

I wanted to touch her, and I felt I dared not.

Reverend Westell stood by patiently. He understood what I experienced in this, my first exposure to the phenomenal Goose Girl Statue. "Oh!" I uttered in a subdued voice, "oh, it is too much! She is too breathtaking!"

"She is, indeed."

After a few moments of being completely overwhelmed, I returned to myself and recalled our assignment. "Are you capturing this, Robbie?" I said into my wrist comp.

"Every moment," he replied.

"Is it truly all right for me to touch her?" I asked the Reverend.

"Oh yes. That is her particular energy, to be touched. To help, heal, and make whole those in need. Or in this instance, to help her. One must understand that she is not organic, but she *is* sentient."

"I understand," I said simply. I approached the Goose Girl Statue, and now I actually began to see the statue itself, instead of only the light and the light's energy. The sweetest, loveliest young woman stood looking down at her little gaggle of three geese, with love glowing in her eyes. And yet more engaging, the look of love the geese, looking up at her, had for her in return.

"The Reverend and I are now going to return you to your place in the church. Thank you for letting me be a part of this spiritual experience," I said. I looked at Reverend Westell, who had put down his umbrella, and stood on the other side of the Goose Girl Statue.

I figured she must weigh around five hundred pounds, and I had a hard time imagining how we could lift her even across the two feet into the car, let alone how we'd get her to her stand in the church. I had a cart at home that would come in handy, and I imagined I might have to get it before we were through.

"Ready?" I asked.

"Can't get ready-ier," he quipped.

"On three. One ... two ... three." I hefted the Goose Girl Statue, only to have almost thrown her to the floor if Reverend Westell hadn't had a strong hold on her.

"She's not a football!" he exclaimed.

"Oh! So very light! I was unprepared!"

"I told you she would assist us."

"I understand, now."

We gently placed the Goose Girl Statue in the back of the car. Then the Reverend closed his storage space doors, retrieved his umbrella, and we climbed into the car.

"Car, please take us back to the church."

"Yes, Dr. Forest." The car hummed merrily the short distance to the church, and without even being instructed, drove to the far side small door, and backed up to the door.

"Very good, Car."

"Thank you."

We got out of the car, went around to the back, and the car opened the hatch door. I opened the little door to the church and peeked in. Enough light came from the stained glass windows and the Goose Girl Statue's stand for us to see.

I came back, and we each took hold of the Goose Girl Statue, then stepped carefully to the little doorway, down the hall, and over to her stand. We placed her on it. I could swear I heard celestial music ... from where?

"Do you hear that?"

"Of course. Approval from other dimensions," Reverend Westell said.

We moved over to the front pew to sit and drink in the incredible, somewhat hard-to-believe, sight before us. The light, though soft and gentle, throbbed to a rhythm of its own paranormal making.

"I shouldn't have taken her," he said.

"Star has made it very clear that she belongs to you."

"In earthly, legal terms, that's true. But, she doesn't belong to me, she belongs to everyone. I took her because there is so much pain where I live, in the retirement home. I wanted to help everyone's unhappiness and physical pain, but people are on their own journey, and many are not open, strange though it may seem, to a spontaneous, miraculous healing."

I nodded. "I can understand that, just a little bit. I got injured yesterday. I came to the residual Goose Girl Statue's light, and it was so strange. I resisted putting my injured fingers in the light. I still don't quite understand it, but I do recall the feeling."

"But you did do it."

"Yes, I did do it. On threat of my robot cat I was connected with, calling someone to come and attend to me. Maybe I didn't feel worthy. Maybe I really didn't believe in it, even though I'd witnessed an amazing healing miracle, and *did* believe in it. But maybe somewhere inside me, I still didn't quite believe it. The whole litany one hears endlessly that there's no such thing as miracles."

"There are *absolutely* such things as miracles," Reverend Westell said. "In my opinion, 'miracles' is simply another word for belief. Belief is tricky business for a lot of people, and I should know as I've been in the business of 'belief' my whole, entire life. Quite a few years now."

"Oh!" I said, "that's insightful and informative ... 'miracles' is another word for belief. Thank you so much, you're a real teacher."

We sat in silent reverie, meditating on the Goose Girl Statue for some time.

Chapter 23
All Wrapped Up in the Moment

Later that day, after Reverend Westell and I had shown Star what we'd done, the three of us were sitting outside sipping tea in the glow of a lovely spring day, among the delighted geese, happy to keep us company with their chatter. They'd been issued into the church by Star to see their beloved Goose Girl Statue returned. They honked and hummed and trilled at the sight, they were so happy to see her, and her beautiful geese at her side!

I loved witnessing their glee.

Then Zev stopped by in his Drago, and not long after, Goldie arrived. I had the strongest feeling that Travis needed to be here as well. Just as I had this thought, he popped up on my wrist comp.

"I was just thinking about you," I said.

"I guess I heard you. What's up?"

"Can you come over to Star's?"

"Are you there again?"

"More like 'still.' But ... can you come?"

"Yeah, I'm off duty. I called to see if you'd like to go out for tea or some-such. This is better. I'll be there shortly."

Everyone having heard the conversation, fell into a kind of silence. Even the geese sat in a cozy group and fell silent, waiting for Travis.

True to his word, he soon drove up in his personal, rather rickety, old as my Forrester, *not* self-driving, vehicle of some nondescript make. The geese leapt up and ran toward him, honking with wings extended, so excited to see him.

Me too. I happened to be facing the parking lot, and I got to see him get out of his car and amble toward us. There he was, in casual street clothes. Not a sight I, or anyone else for that matter, often had the privilege of seeing.

He looked spectacular. He came and stood over our table, taking in each of our faces in turn. "A bunch of cats who've eaten canaries," he said.

"Have a seat," Star gestured to the empty chair beside me.

"All right." He noticed the little teapot and tiny tea cups. "Are we having rose petal tea?"

"By a landslide vote in the affirmative, yes, it's rose petal tea," Zev said, laughing.

"Would you like some?" Star asked.

"I would," Travis said.

Star poured Travis a cup of tea. "There are also these little cookies I made. They're not rose petal cookies, but everyone seems to like them. Would you like some?"

"Absolutely." Travis held out his saucer, and Star put half-a-dozen little cookies on it.

"Love them!" Goldie said.

"Yes, yes," the men agreed. "Love them."

Travis bit into one and sipped his tea. "Oh, heavenly. Thank you for inviting me, Joy. But … what's the occasion?" He turned to Reverend Westell. "I believe I don't know this gentleman."

"This is the Reverend William Westell," Star said. "He used to be the pastor of this church."

Travis reached across the little table and shook his hand. "Nice to meet you, Reverend." He looked around at each of us, gradually raising his eyebrows. "No really, something is going on."

"Yes Travis, You're quite perceptive," I said. "We're having a little tea party, celebrating the fact that the Goose Girl Statue has been returned."

"Oh!" Travis exclaimed. "That's big news! You're all extremely casual for something so significant. Tell me more."

"Well, you see, yesterday, I couldn't find the peanut butter...." I said.

"You ... couldn't find the peanut butter... How's that?..."

"I couldn't find the peanut butter, but it was right in front of me when Robbie pointed it out to me. All day long I had a haunting thought that the mystery of the Goose Girl Statue was like the peanut butter, with the answer right in front of my eyes. I was looking at it, and didn't see it.

"Then last night Star said, 'the statue has been moved without having been stolen.' I took it to mean what she has been saying, that she believed it had apported.

"But while I finished the inventory of the religious relics, that comment of hers kept rolling around in my mind. When I finished, I stepped out in the glorious pre-dawn morning, and saw the Reverend down the hill, on his way to come to the church. But when he saw my car, he turned around.

"So I went down the hill and, one might say, I rather much stalked him. I found him at his storage space at his apartment complex, where sat the Goose Girl Statue.

"As I came up to him, I heard him say he wished he could return her to the church. He'd taken it by renting a vehicle, which had just about done him in, and he was overwhelmed at the thought of returning it.

"I appeared before him at that moment! We brought Goose Girl Statue back this morning. This answered the question of how the statue could be taken without being stolen, as it belongs to the Reverend."

"But, Star, did you tell her about how the Goose Girl Statue came to be here in the first place?"

"I don't think so, no."

"She apported. When I owned the church, and I had a huge congregation—three services on Sunday and one on Saturday evening, it was lovely! It's lovely now, as well, of course, saving the animals and healing people and pets. However, one Sunday morning, I came in before the first service, and the Goose Girl Statue stood where she is now. Just ... apported."

"So it was logical for me to think she apported again," Star added.

"Did you truly not know Reverend Westell had her?" Travis asked.

"No. I didn't. I didn't even think of it. He could come and go here as he pleased, so the thought didn't cross my mind."

"But, you see," Reverend Westell continued, "where I live, there are so many sick and depressed people. I had the completely erroneous thought that if the statue was closer to them, they would heal. But, of course, distance has nothing to do with it. I had to learn that some people simply have to go through their own journey with pain and sadness. They aren't ready to believe in a miracle. Instead ... another miracle happened."

"What was that?" Travis asked, curious, practically on the edge of his seat. I loved seeing him out of his total coolness, all wrapped up in the moment.

"Why, the appearance of Joy, of course! If you consider the intricate trajectory of fate, for her to end up at my place this morning when, I had finally decided, *at that very moment!* that the Goose Girl Statue had to be returned, there she was."

Travis looked over at me, head cocked, half smiling. "She does seem to have that particular ... miraculous ... ability."

"Why, thank you, Detective Rusch," I said.

"Just stating the facts. Mystical sometimes, though they may be."

Travis and Reverend Westell became engaged in a conversation about the Reverend's history in the community. This was one of the areas where Travis and I intersected. We were both fascinated by culture, whether local or distant, it took our attention.

Meanwhile, I couldn't help overhearing a bit of conversation between Star and Zev on my other side.

"I have a confession," Zev said in a quiet, slightly guilty-sounding voice.

"Oh?" Star answered, cool-as-a-cucumber. "What's that?"

"I saw you at Larry's the other day."

"You did?" Her surprise was unrestrained. "But ... I don't understand. I didn't see you."

"No. I came to the door, and I saw you there, head to head with Larry, And I ... I turned away and hurried off before you could see me."

"But why, Zev? Why?"

"Because I didn't know... you know, you and he, and ... I didn't know."

"Why did you go there?"

"I was going to ask him to watch for the Goose Girl Statue."

"Really? You were?" she asked, candid surprise in her voice.

"Don't sound so surprised."

"But I *am* surprised. I didn't know you'd do something like that for me."

"Of course, I would. If it's important to you, it's important to me. But you know, about Larry...."

"There's nothing 'about Larry,' Zev. He's a friend. That's all. He called me to come look at a holo of a statue that wasn't the Goose Girl Statue at all. In fact, It made me rather irritated with him. You can ask Joy, she drove me down and brought me back home. She got to hear about my frustration about a trip for no reason."

"Not 'no reason.' The reason being he's still in love with you."

"Not to sound heartless, but that's not my problem. Maybe it's love, and maybe it's a sort of codependent enmeshment. Do you not feel secure about how I feel for you?"

"No, not entirely. But you must know by now, Star, I'm not secure about anything." He chuckled self-deprecatingly.

"Continuing in the vein of candid revelation, Zev, your self-judgment is also not my problem. You must grow through it and learn what's to be learned. I cannot do it for you. No one can do it for you."

"You're right, Star. But you're so amazing, so beautiful, So...."

"No, Zev, I'm not beautiful."

He laughed. "Now we come to *your* insecurities. I think you're beautiful. I don't think you get to disagree with me about my opinion. If you can't see your beauty, I'll see it for you."

"Hey, where'd you go?" Travis asked me, taking me away from their conversation.

"Oh! Nowhere. I'm right here." I took a long sip of my wonderful tea.

"If it's not too obvious, I'd like to see the Goose Girl Statue," Travis said.

"Oh! But of course! Let's go." We stood. "Travis wants to see the Goose Girl Statue."

"Of course, of course," everyone chorused.

We walked to the church, with the geese happily following us.

"Do we let them in?" Travis asked when we got to the little door.

"Sophia told me they like to be near the statue."

I held the door open. The geese looked at us, and looked back at Star. Then they decided to flap and fly back to her.

"So much like people," Travis said, chuckling. "Never knowing their minds."

"The geese seem to be a lot like people in many ways," I observed.

We stepped inside. The fabulous glow of the Goose Girl Statue bathed the entire front of the church, while the flowing colors of the stained glass windows seemed to fill up the nave to the brim.

"Wow!" Travis whispered.

I led him to the Goose Girl Statue. "Oh!" he said, sounding shocked.

"Oh, what?" I asked, taking my eyes from the adorable and profoundly engaging statue to look at Travis.

"I ... it's ... I ... words fail me. There's more than a light, more than this stunning statue...."

He moved to sit in the front pew, unable to take his eyes off the light. I moved to sit by him.

"It's the emotion," I said.

"Yes. There's an intense evocation of an emotion."

"It's love."

Travis sat in quiet reflection, contemplating what I'd said. "That's what it is. It's love," he whispered, turning to look at me. *Oh, those eyes!*

Everyone, including the geese, chose this moment to come pouring through the little door to join us, chattering and cheerful.

We turned to them, smiling, glowing in the Goose Girl's light of love.

The End

Dear Readers:

I hope you've enjoyed reading *A Gaggle of Geese* as much as I enjoyed writing it. As you may have noticed, I like to include artwork in my books. Although I knew there was Victorian art depicting girls and young women with their geese, I was surprised to discover *how much* wonderful Victorian Goose Girl art there is.

It's been a delight to include a little window of that beautiful, historic art in *A Gaggle of Geese* chapter headings, along with the first and last chapter headings of my own glorious geese. The art and pictures are full color in the ebook version of *A Gaggle of Geese*, and black and white in the paperback, large print, and hardbound versions. Which chapter headings do you like the most?

I usually include the first two chapters of the next *Joy Forest Cozy Mystery*. But at this moment those chapters are not polished. *So!* Instead, I'm giving away an *entire book* as a thank you for reading *A Gaggle of Geese.*

The Darling Undesirables is the first book in my post steampunk, science-fiction series. Yes, it's a different sort of book, but give it a go and let me know what you think. I'd love any feedback you have, sent to me, or Amazon star rating or review.

If you'd like the free ebook, send your request for *The Darling Undesirables* to:

Blythe@BlytheAyne.com

About the Author:

Thank you for reading ***A Gaggle of Geese***. Be sure to read all of Joy Forest's mysterious adventures, which take place in the world of the near future.

Here's a bit about me, if you're curious. I live near where Joy lives, but I'm in the present, about ten years before where Joy's story begins. Unless you're reading this ten years from now, and then, well, I'm in the past, and you're in Joy's present.

I live in the midst (and often the mist) of ten acres of forest, with domestic and wild creatures as family and companions. Here I create an ever-growing inventory of fiction and nonfiction books, short stories, illustrated kid's books, vast amounts of poetry, and the occasional article. I've also begun audio recording my books, which, having a background in performance, I find quite enjoyable.

I throw a bit of wood carving in when I need a change of pace. And I'm frequently on a ladder, cleaning my gutters. There's something spectacular about being on a ladder—the vista opens up all around, and one feels rather like a bird or a squirrel, perched on a metal branch.

After I received my Doctorate from the University of California at Irvine in the School of Social Sciences, (majoring in psychology and ethnography—surprisingly similar to Joy's scholarly background), I moved to the Pacific Northwest to write and to have a modest private psychotherapy practice in a small town not much bigger than a village.

Finally, I decided it was time to put my full focus on my writing, where, through the world-shrinking internet, I could "meet" greater numbers of people. *Where I could meet you!*

All the creatures in my forest and I are glad you "stopped by." Thank you so much for any reviews or comments you may share. We writers create in a void, and hearing from *YOU* makes all the difference.

Blythe@BlytheAyne.com

And here's my website, and my *Boutique of Books*:

www.BlytheAyne.com

https://shop.BlytheAyne.com

'Til We Meet Again,

Blythe

Notations on the Art:

Made in the USA
Las Vegas, NV
17 February 2023

67674544R00121